JAILBREAK!

"Ralls!" a man cried out. "He's escaped from jail!"

As he heard the shout, Ralls cursed softly, then started across the street, running. He was nearing his horses when he saw the restaurant door open, and Ella Snow appeared in the doorway.

Ralls reached his horses and was vaulting into the saddle when Les Cagle appeared in the doorway of the sheriff's office with a shotgun in his hands.

In the act of mounting, Ralls didn't see Cagle. But Ella saw and cried out: "Look out, Jim!" But her warning came too late, as Cagle lifted the shotgun and blazed away at the helpless Ralls. . . .

⊘ Signet Brand Western

The Lone Gunhawk

by
Frank Gruber

also published as:
SMOKY ROAD

A SIGNET BOOK

NEW AMERICAN LIBRARY

PUBLISHED BY
PENGUIN BOOKS CANADA LIMITED

PUBLISHER'S NOTE

This book is a work of fiction. Names, characters, places, and incidents are either the product of the author's imagination or are used fictitiously, and any resemblance to actual persons, living or dead, events, or locales is entirely coincidental.

Copyright © 1947, 1948, 1949 by Frank Gruber

Copyright © renewed 1976 by Mrs. Lois Gruber

All rights reserved. For information address Mrs. Lois Gruber c/o New American Library.

Published by arrangement with Mrs. Lois Gruber

First Signet Printing, January, 1983

4 5 6 7 8 9 10 11

SIGNET TRADEMARK REG. U.S. PAT. OFF AND FOREIGN COUNTRIES
REGISTERED TRADEMARK — MARCA REGISTRADA
HECHO EN WINNIPEG, CANADA

SIGNET, SIGNET CLASSIC, MENTOR, ONYX, PLUME, MERIDIAN and NAL BOOKS are published in Canada by Penguin Books Canada Limited, 2801 John Street, Markham, Ontario, Canada L3R 1B4
PRINTED IN CANADA
COVER PRINTED IN U.S.A.

One

AN EMIGRANT train, seeking the shortcut to the golden land on the Pacific Coast, had once toiled up the eastern slope of this mountain and looking down the almost vertical western side had abandoned all hope. One member of the train had blown out his brains and had been buried here on the crest of the mountain.

The wooden cross that marked the rocky grave was weathered and rotting and in a few years more would be gone.

Ralls, dismounting a few feet from the old wooden cross, barely glanced at it. He had seen other crosses and sometimes when the graves had been shallow he had seen bones. The West had taken many lives and some day it would take the life of Jim Ralls.

Perhaps the valley below would be Ralls' resting place. For Ralls, unlike the emigrants, had no intention of turning back from this spot. He had no wagons, no women or children to get down this precipitous mountainside. He had only himself and his two horses, the eighteen-year-old black gelding he rode and the shaggy-looking pack horse that carried his gear. And they were as sure-footed as mountain sheep.

The valley, from where Ralls stood, looked like a vast

horseshoe. A haze that hung above the ground concealed the floor of the valley, but Ralls, judging from the green slopes of the mountainside, thought that the valley would be green, too.

He took down the canteen from his saddle pommel and drank a small quantity of water. Then drawing a deep breath, he mounted the old horse and started it down the steep mountainside. The animal picked its way carefully, testing doubtful spots with a forefoot before putting its full weight on them. Behind it came the pack horse, following its mate but with less sureness.

The descent was a slow one. Several times Ralls was compelled to dismount and proceed on foot ahead of the gelding. He was negotiating a particularly bad stretch when the sudden report of a gun below him caused him to stiffen.

Another shot was fired and then a third and Ralls moved swiftly around his gelding so that its body shielded him, but in that position he realized that the shooting had not been directed at him. He came out from behind his horse and, looking down, saw figures moving about, several hundred yards below.

Even as he watched, there was a fusillade of gunfire below and the sound of angry voices came to his ears.

Twenty feet below Ralls was a narrow shelf of rocky shale. His eyes followed it and he saw that it widened considerably as it fell rapidly down into the valley.

Ralls descended to the shelf and waited a moment until his animals caught up with him. Then he mounted the gelding and urged it forward. It followed the shelf at a brisk pace for several minutes until the shelf petered out into grassy mountain slope, at an easier angle than any they had traversed so far.

Several shots were fired below as they traveled along the shelf, but they became fainter, as the shelf led Ralls away from the scene of the shooting. But now, since he was traveling down an easier grade, he turned his horse back in the direction of the shooting.

A few minutes later he pulled up in the shelter of several trees and looked out upon a scene of violence. Four men, armed with rifles and pistols, were converging upon a fifth man who had taken shelter behind a fallen pine tree and who had been outflanked and wounded. The man was standing up behind the fallen tree trunk and was yelling defiance at his enemies, at the same time he was emptying his gun at them; this last with rather poor effect, inasmuch as his right arm hung limp at his side and he was shooting with his left hand.

One of the attackers suddenly skidded to a halt, threw up a rifle, took aim, and fired.

The pistol flew from the already wounded man's left hand and he fell forward across the tree trunk that had been his barricade. The four men swarmed over him.

Wounded and disarmed, he still struggled with his captors but a rope was thrown about his waist and he was dragged across the rough ground to a standing pine tree, some twenty yards away.

There he was yanked to his feet, the rope taken from about his waist and the end of it thrown over a low-hanging limb. One of the men began fashioning a hangman's noose with the other end of the rope.

It was then that Ralls came out from his vantage spot and put his gelding into a swift trot.

The men ahead were so intent on their work that Ralls came within fifty yards of them before he was discovered. One of the men snatched up his rifle then and pointed it at Ralls. But Ralls ignored the gun. He rode up to within a dozen paces of the group before halting.

The man with the rifle moved forward, still keeping Ralls covered. "All right, stranger," he said, "you can just keep riding along."

"Why," said Ralls, "I've been riding

thought I'd rest a spell." He nodded to the wounded man. "Little hanging?"

A second man stepped up beside the rifleman. He was a huge, heavy-jowled man in his early thirties. "Nothin' you'd be interested in, stranger," he said. "Just a rustler."

"That's a lie!" cried the captive. That was as far as he got, for the man fashioning the hangman's noose struck him in the face with the rope-end.

"Keep your trap shut!" he snarled. He hit the wounded man a second time and was drawing back for a third blow when Ralls' voice rang out:

"I wouldn't do that again!"

The man with the rope ran forward. "Why, goddam you, I'll give you some of the same."

Ralls raised both of his hands to shoulder height, palms turned outward so that the men on the ground could see his empty hands. He swung his left foot over the saddle pommel and jumped lightly to the ground. He still held up his hands.

"All right," he challenged. "Give it to me."

The man with the rope was about to do just that, but the heavy-jowled man gestured him back. He said, to Ralls: "It's just as easy to hang two men as one."

Ralls' body shifted slightly so that his left side was forward. He said quietly: "There'll be no hangings today."

A hush fell upon the group. It was broken by the man with the rope. He said: "Mister, you asked for it . . ."

He suddenly let the rope fall from his hand. At the same time the hand shot for the gun that swung from his hip in a well-worn holster. The gun cleared leather—and then Ralls' hands came down. His right was a mere blur as it sped for the low-slung Navy gun at his thigh. Starting a split second after the other man, Ralls beat him with time to spare. His bullet caught the man squarely in the center of his In almost the same movement Ralls threw him and fired again, this time at the heavy-jowled man. The bullet tore through the man's left arm and threw him off balance.

The other two men were touching their guns as Ralls shifted quickly and covered them.

Ralls said: "I said there'd be no hangings today."

The men were stunned. The mouth of one of them moved and had to move a second time before words came forth: "Gawd," the man said, "I never saw such drawin'. . . ."

"An' shootin'," added the other man who had not been wounded.

But the heavy-jowled man gripped his wounded arm with his other hand and looked down at the dead man. His face was dark with hot blood.

"You'll rue this day's work," he said thickly, to Ralls. "You can't ride fast enough, or far enough, to get away from this."

"As to that," Ralls said, "you'd better get on your horse and start riding yourself." He gestured to the other two men. "And that goes for you, too."

Then the wounded man, whom the others had wanted to hang, staggered forward. "Wait a minute, stranger," he cried. "You can't let them go." He bent down to scoop up the gun the heavy-jowled man had dropped, but Ralls stepped forward quickly and kicked the gun out of his reach.

The wounded man exclaimed, "Mister, what he said is true. They'll follow you wherever you go." He pointed down at the dead man. "This one's Kirby Jenkins"—he stabbed a forefinger at the wounded man—"Reb Jenkins' brother."

"I'll remember the name," Ralls said.

"Do that," Reb Jenkins gritted through his teeth.

Ralls ignored him. He looked at the other two men. "You want me to remember your names?"

The two men exchanged glances and Ralls saw fear in

their eyes. One of them shook his head. "We only work for the H-L."

"Why, you yellow-livered cowards!" cried Reb Jenkins. "You were just as keen on hangin' Ellis as anyone, but this man throws a fancy gun on you and you start shakin' in your goddam boots." He sneered at Ralls. "I'll tell you their names; the skinny one calls himself Hack Butler and the other one's Fred Anson and you won't find them at the H-L because they won't be working there after today."

And with that Reb Jenkins stalked off. Butler and Anson hesitated, looked worriedly at Jim Ralls, then started off. But Ralls gestured them back. "You're forgetting your partner." He nodded to the dead man.

The two cowboys turned back and, picking up the dead man between them, lumbered off toward their horses, which were tied to trees some distance down the slope.

Ellis, the wounded man, watched them go. "That's a mistake," he said bitterly to Ralls. "Butler and Anson don't amount to much, but Reb Jenkins is the ramrod of the H-L and you know what that means."

"I don't," Ralls said.

"I meant the H-L Ranch."

"Is the H-L Ranch supposed to mean something?"

The wounded man looked at him in astonishment. "Where're you from, mister?"

Ralls looked up the mountain slope. "The other side."

"How far on the other side: The H-L is known wherever there's cattle."

"Oh, that ranch," Ralls said, although he had never heard of it. "It's something, then?"

"You'll find out. Harley Langford never forgets and he never forgives. He . . ." Ellis suddenly stopped. His eyes closed in pain and he swayed on his feet. Ralls, stepping forward quickly, caught him as he collapsed in a dead faint.

*   *   *

When the sun was high in the heavens Ralls built the tiniest of fires and broiled some bacon. Using water from his canteen he made coffee. He ate the bacon and was drinking the coffee when the wounded man began to groan and roll restlessly from side to side under the blanket with which Ralls had covered him. Ralls carried the tin cup of coffee to the man and, raising his head, poured some of the liquid into his mouth.

Ellis coughed and choked, but his eyes opened. For a moment they looked blankly into Ralls', then he struggled to sit up. "I've got to go," he exclaimed. "I've got to be riding."

"You'll do no riding . . . today. . . ."

"I've got to, mister. You saved my life, but it ain't goin' to be no good if I don't get into a saddle and start ridin'. . . ."

"You've lost a lot of blood," Ralls said, "you've got a slug in your chest and one in your arm. If you'll tell me where you live, I'll ride over—"

"No!" Ellis cried. "There's nobody there and you'd only—you'd only be letting them know that I . . ."

He began to cough and Ralls handed him the coffee. It was poor medicine, but Ralls, who had seen many wounded men in his time, did not think it made any difference.

Ellis drank the coffee, then let his head fall back to the ground. He looked at the sky a moment, then rolled his head sidewards.

"I'll rest a half hour, then climb into the saddle. . . ."

"I don't think you can make it."

"I've got a chance," Ellis said, stubbornly, "but if sunup finds me here in the valley I'm a goner. I know Langford and his son Emmett and I know Reb Jenkins and Sam Sloane—"

"Sam Sloane?"

"He works for Langford. You know him?"

"I've heard the name."

"Worst man in the West; the fastest gun-slinger, except maybe Jim Ralls."

Kneeling, Ralls leaned back and rested his haunches on his heels. He regarded the dying man a moment. "This Ralls . . . he's known in the valley?"

"Where isn't he known? Nobody knows anything about him. Nobody knows him—except the men he's killed."

Ralls did not speak for a moment. Then he said: "You've heard about a lot of people, Ellis. I wonder if you've ever heard of a man named Martindale—Rance Martindale?"

Ellis started to shake his head, then stopped. "Martindale," he whispered. "Rance Martindale . . ." Then suddenly his eyes widened. "Yes! Martindale. . . ."

Like a striking rattlesnake, Ralls lunged forward and gripped the wounded man's arm so savagely that Ellis winced in pain. "Where've you heard the name?" he cried.

"Let go!" gasped Ellis. "You're hurting." Ralls dropped the arm he was gripping.

"Tell me, Ellis!"

"I'm trying to think," Ellis said, heavily. "I—I almost had it, but I can't concentrate. The pain—"

Ralls groaned. "Think, Ellis—think hard."

"I'm . . . trying . . ." gasped Ellis. A spasm of pain shook his weakened body. His eyes tightened, then relaxed and finally closed. Ralls leaned quickly over, felt his heart. It was still beating, but weakly.

Ralls drank some more coffee and put out the little fire. Then, turning to look at the wounded man he saw his eyes open and watching him. He crossed and dropped to one knee.

"You're Ralls, aren't you?" Ellis asked suddenly. "You're the man who's been going around for years asking people about Rance Martindale. . . ."

"I'm the man," Ralls said, "but that isn't how you've heard about Martindale."

"It's all mixed up. I—I thought I'd heard the name years ago, before I heard of Ralls, but I'm not so sure now. It wasn't a name anyone talked about. You heard it only in a whisper and whoever said it would usually pretend he didn't know what you were talking about later."

"You're dying, Ellis," Ralls said, bluntly. "This is not time to be holding things back."

"I'm getting out of here, Ralls, or whatever your name is. In a little while when I've rested, I'm going to ride—"

"You'll never ride again!"

Ellis' face twisted spasmodically. "I should have kept my mouth shut. I shouldn't have told you a thing. All right, you saved my life, but . . ." He stopped, agony on his face.

Alarm, Ralls grabbed hold of the dying man. "You're going, Ellis. You can't hold back. I've hunted too long. You've got to tell me . . ."

Bloody froth appeared on Ellis' lips. His mouth worked horribly, then suddenly fell open. His eyes remained wide open, but were sightless. With a groan, Ralls let the dead body sink back upon the ground.

Ellis was dead and Ralls had learned nothing from him. Nothing, except that Rance Martindale had once been known in this vicinity.

Later Ralls scooped out a shallow grave and buried Ellis. Then with a tree branch he swished away all marks of the grave. It was almost sundown when he finally mounted his horse and rode away.

Two

—————•••—————

AN HOUR later Ralls' nostrils sniffed smoke. He searched the widening valley for the source of it, but it wasn't until he had passed a large grove of cottonwoods that he saw it, the smoldering ruins of a ranch house, a half mile to the south. He swerved his horse in that direction. A corral remained standing, but only smoking logs remained in several spots; the largest pile indicated where the house had stood, the others barns and outbuildings. A few head of cattle grazed a hundred yards away.

Ralls searched the vicinity but saw no humans. There was a clump of cottonwoods off to the left, however, that worried Ralls. He gave it a rather wide berth as he rode down upon the remains of the ranch buildings.

He rode clear around the charred logs, studying the tracks of horses, sorting them out from the imprints of Ellis' cattle. It was difficult drawing any conclusion, but Ralls' life had often depended upon his knowledge of trails and tracks and the significance of them. He got the impression now that there had been no attack upon the ranch at all. Ellis had either fled at the approach of the riders or had been away at the time. Hoofprints showed no unusual galloping back and forth, at least not the newer hoofprints.

10

They came down boldly upon the buildings, had circled them, and gone here and there, with deliberation.

Ralls sat his mount, studying the situation. He seemed relaxed in his saddle, but he was aware of everything. The flitting glint of a long sunbeam upon steel caused him to throw himself sidewards from the saddle.

Off in the cottonwoods a rifle banged and a bullet whined over the saddle of Ralls' mount. Had he still been sitting in it, the bullet would have hit him.

Hitting the ground, Ralls whirled, lunged for the rifle in the saddle scabbard. He whipped it out, poked it across the saddle and fired a quick shot into the woods.

There was a heavy thrashing in the cottonwoods. Ralls sprang into the saddle of his horse, turned it toward the woods. The animal leaped forward. Bending low in the saddle, Ralls levered a fresh cartridge into the chamber of his rifle. Fifty yards from the edge of the cottonwoods he suddenly swerved his horse and sent it at breakneck speed skirting the trees. As he made the turn, Ralls sent a second bullet crashing into the trees.

The ruse worked. The man in the woods thought that the pursuit was coming after him, straight through the trees. But Ralls, riding his gelding at top speed clear around the five-acre tract of cottonwoods, caught the horseman as he burst out of the woods.

The man saw Ralls from a distance of less than a hundred feet, cried out in alarm and fright. And then Ralls' third rifle bullet cut him from the saddle. The man hit the ground heavily, turned a complete somersault and thrashed about on the ground.

Riding up, Ralls dismounted and approached the wounded man. He was badly hit, but seeing Ralls he made a feeble attempt to draw his revolver. Ralls kicked it from his hand.

"What's your name?" Ralls demanded.

"Go—to—hell!" was the reply.

"That's where you're going," Ralls replied grimly. "In just a few minutes. . . ."

The man cursed horribly, but it was obvious that he knew he was going.

"Ever hear of a man named Rance Martindale?" Ralls persisted. The man began to sob, but after a moment quieted down. His eyes met Ralls'.

"W-who?" he asked.

"Rance Martindale. Ever hear of him?"

The man shook his head. "You're—you're one of Langford's gunnies. . . ."

Ralls' eyes narrowed. Then suddenly he dropped to one knee. "Aren't you an H-L man?"

"Me?" The man on the ground gasped. "I thought you . . ." He stopped.

"Reb Jenkins and his crew burned Ellis' place," Ralls said. "And killed Ellis. They're Langford men. . . ."

"I know."

"And aren't you one of them?"

The man started to shake his head, but seemed too weak to make the movement. "Then why'd you shoot at me?" Ralls snapped.

"D-don't you know?" the man asked.

"Of course not. I'm a stranger here. I rode down on a hanging bee and saved Ellis. He was wounded, but even then—even then he wouldn't talk. Like you. You're dying and still—"

"Dying?" gasped the man. "Who's dying . . . ?" And then a groan came from his throat and he was gone.

Ralls got to his feet, looked down bitterly at the dead man, drew a deep breath and turned to his horse.

Ralls slept out that night under the stars, but with sunup he was in the saddle. After riding awhile he struck a trail which in time became a rutted road. In mid-morning he saw a ranch house and corrals off to the left and the rutted road converged with another and became a well-beaten highway.

An hour later, Ralls rode into the outskirts of a town. It consisted of a wide, tree-shaded street of two or three blocks in length. Horses were tied to the hitchrails and a few people looked covertly at Ralls as he rode down the street. Ralls got the impression that he was expected.

He dismounted in front of a one-story building that had a sign *Cagle's Place* over the false front, and a smaller one over the door, on which was painted a glass of beer.

He tied the horses to the hitchrail and ducked underneath to enter the saloon. A heavy-set man, who was leaning against the building beside the door, spat out a stream of tobacco juice.

"Hi, stranger," he said casually.

Ralls nodded. "Hello."

He went into the saloon. It was a big, cool room, furnished with tables and a long bar down one side. A bartender was polishing glasses behind the bar. The only other occupant of the room was a lean, sardonic man who sat at the far end of the bar, figuring accounts.

Ralls went up to the bar. "A glass of beer," he said.

The bartender finished polishing a glass and then drew a beer. Ralls quaffed it thirstily. As he set the glass on the bar, the man who had greeted him outside came into the saloon and stopped beside Ralls. He signaled to the bartender. "Two beers, Herman."

The bartender removed Ralls' empty glass and brought two beers. The man beside Ralls picked up one of the glasses and saluted him.

"A good trip," he said.

Ralls drank a little of the beer and set the glass on the bar. "It was all right."

The other man pursed his lips. "I meant the trip from here on."

"I was thinking of resting awhile."

"That mightn't be such a good idea."

"Why not?"

The other man shrugged. "Reb Jenkins brought in his brother. Reb had a bullet in his arm hisself."

"Did he tell you how he got it?"

"Yes. Said he had a brush with some rustlers." The heavy-set man drank some beer. "Reb's foreman of the H-L."

Ralls nodded. "A good man, too, isn't he?"

"Depends on what you mean by good. If you mean a good enemy, yes, Reb's a good man. And a good fighter, too." He frowned at his empty beer glass. "I don't wear a badge because everybody around here knows I'm the sheriff." He cleared his throat. "Fred Cherry."

Ralls nodded acknowledgment of the introduction. "I suppose Reb told you that he and his brother and a couple of men were going to hang a man?"

"Just a rustler."

"All right, a rustler. But I thought even rustlers got a trial before a judge and sometimes a jury."

"Oh, they do. Meadowlands is a county seat and we've got a judge right here. But this is cattle country and cattlemen being what they are, well . . ." The sheriff squinted. "You got me off the subject. What I started to say was, things are quiet here in Meadowlands and I wouldn't want any shootin' so, like I was sayin', it'd be best if you just kept on riding. With Reb Jenkins gunnin' for you, none of the other ranchers would want to hire you anyway, so there wouldn't be any point in hanging around here, would there?"

"Not if I was looking for a job, no."

"Aren't you?"

"I'm looking—but not for a job."

Sheriff Cherry squinted again at his empty glass and discovering that it was empty, signaled to Herman the bartender. "Fill 'em up."

Ralls put a half dollar on the bar. "Mine, this time."

"Oh, thanks, thanks, Mister . . . ?"

But Ralls didn't respond to the invitation to give his name. He said: "The H-L Ranch—it's a big outfit?"

"Biggest in the state. Eighty thousand acres of the finest grass in the country. Sixty thousand head of cattle. Folks been tryin' to get Langford to run for governor. Says he can't afford the time, but we hope he'll let us run him just the same."

At the end of the bar, the lean man looked up from his accounts. "You talk too much with your mouth, Cherry."

The sheriff gave a start. "Guess I do." He swallowed some beer, got some in his windpipe and choked until the tears ran down his cheeks. Ralls watched him dispassionately.

While the sheriff was still coughing, the door opened and a man stepped in. It was Anson, one of the men Reb Jenkins had denounced the day before. He saw Ralls and his mouth fell open. Then he clamped it shut, wheeled and popped out of the saloon again.

Ralls picked up his twenty cents change, dropped it into a pocket and, nodding to the red-faced sheriff, headed for the door. He went through and on the wooden sidewalk outside stopped with his back to the saloon door.

Across the street, Anson was talking to a couple of cowboys, one a young man in his early twenties, the other a weather-beaten veteran. Talking animatedly, Anson chanced to look across the street and spied Ralls. He almost jumped, so quickly did he break away from the men he was talking to.

Anson ran into a store and the two men he had left started across the street toward Ralls.

Ralls stood at the edge of the wooden sidewalk, his feet planted wide apart, his hands dangling at his sides. The two men approached him, the younger man slightly ahead of his companion. He stopped in the street, ten feet from Ralls.

"You're the man killed Kirby Jenkins," he accused.

Ralls said: "Go home, son."

The man's face twisted. "I'm Emmett Langford. My father owns the H-L. Kirby worked for us and—"

"—and so did Reb," Ralls flashed at him. "And Anson and Butler."

"You sneaked up on them," Emmett Langford snarled. "You got the drop on them and you shot down Kirby Jenkins in cold blood."

"And his brother, too," snapped Ralls. "Don't be a fool, boy. Anson's across the street; ask him how I sneaked up. Ask him before you make the last mistake of your life."

Emmett surveyed Ralls without conviction. "Fancy yourself as a gun-slinger, do you?"

Diagonally across the street, a girl wearing Levis and a flannel shirt came out of a store and mounted a buckskin horse. She looked over in the direction of Ralls and the two men facing him. Then she whirled her horse and sent him galloping across the street toward them.

Ralls heard the pounding of the horse's hoofs, but kept his eyes on the men before him.

Behind Emmett the older man crowded forward. "Looky here, stranger," he said, "there's two of us and—"

His words were drowned by the clamor of the galloping horse, which shot forward and was jerked to an abrupt halt between Emmett Langford and Jim Ralls.

The girl's eyes were blazing. "Emmett!" she cried. "Stop it."

"Get away from here, Sage," Emmett Langford growled. "This is the man who bushwhacked Kirby and Reb Jenkins."

"I don't care who he is," the girl called Sage said. "You're not going to fight him."

"I can take care of myself," Emmett Langford snarled.

"No, you can't," the girl said. "You can't fight a man

like—like him.'' She whirled on Ralls. ''And you, taunting a mere boy into a fight.''

''I told him to go home,'' Ralls said.

''I'm not afraid of you,'' Emmett cried. ''And don't you go talking to me like I was a kid.''

''I'd just as soon not talk to you at all,'' Ralls retorted.

Enraged, young Langford tried to step around the girl's horse to get at Ralls. But the girl kneed the horse forward and it knocked Langford to one side. At the same time she jerked the animal's head around and drove it up on the wooden sidewalk. Ralls was compelled to step aside nimbly and the girl struck at him with her riding whip, a stinging blow that seared Ralls' face.

Ralls exclaimed and retreated, but the wall of the saloon brought him up short. The girl pressed forward and struck at him again and a third time. Then she suddenly whirled her horse and began beating young Langford with the whip.

''And that's for you,'' she cried. ''And if it isn't enough I'll tell Dad and you'll catch some more.''

Emmett Langford cried out with each blow and finally, with Sage pursuing him, he broke and ran across the street. The girl followed, raining blows upon his head and shoulders. Langford finally took refuge in a store and the girl turned her horse for a final survey of the situation. Ralls promptly stepped into Cagle's saloon.

Inside he collided with the sardonic Cagle, who had been watching the scene over the top of the batwing doors.

''Nice fun,'' the saloonkeeper commented.

Ralls rubbed his smarting face. ''Some people might think so.''

''You've seen a fair sample of the Langfords,'' Cagle said.

''The girl's young Langford's sister?''

''Yes and no. Emmett isn't really Langford's son, although he's brought him up like he was. He picked up the kid after the Mountain Meadow Massacre.''

"That was seventeen years ago," Ralls said. "I didn't know this country was settled at that time."

"Oh, it wasn't. Langford stopped here right after the Massacre. I guess he was here for three-four years before anyone else settled here." Cagle paused a moment. "That's how he happened to get the valley."

"He just took it?"

Cagle shrugged. "He was strong enough to hold it."

Three

SAGE LANGFORD halted her horse on the grassy knoll and looked down at the cottonwoods which sheltered and shaded the buildings of the H-L Ranch. The long rambling white house had been her home for seventeen of her twenty-one years. She knew every inch of the ranch yard that surrounded the house. She had climbed the corrals from childhood, had explored the barns and stables, even the quarters of the cowboys. Her life here had been a happy one. Happy until recently.

Even now she found it hard to say just what was wrong. But that there was something wrong she was positive. She sensed it in the booming of her father's voice. She knew it from the wildness of Emmett, her brother; he had always been headstrong, but lately he was wilder than ever. And the cowboys, always calm, were calmer now.

Well, today she would have it out with her father.

She drove her filly into an easy lope and rode down to the ranch buildings. At the corrals she dismounted and threw the reins to a bowlegged cowboy.

"Where's Dad?" she asked.

The cowboy nodded toward a flat-roofed white building. "In his office, I guess."

Sage strode toward the building, slapping her doeskin

boots with her riding whip. As she walked with long
strides she looked more like a boy than ever, except for
her golden hair, which cascaded over her shoulders, although it was supposed to be tied down with a hair ribbon.

Near the office building was a gnarled old cottonwood
tree, under which was a circular wooden bench. Reb Jenkins,
his left arm supported in a bandana sling, got up from the
bench.

"Here you are, Sage," he said gruffly.

"Yes," Sage retorted, without slackening her pace.

Reb scowled. "Where've you been?"

"Minding my own business."

The foreman stepped in her path. "You can save that
for someone else. You'n me are going to have a talk . . ."

By that time Sage came up and started to circle him, but
the foreman of the H-L lunged out with his uninjured hand
and grabbed Sage's wrist. She stopped and fixed him with
a cold glance.

"Let go of my arm!"

He hesitated for a moment, but released her. "Gettin'
kinda high and mighty, aren't you?" he asked sullenly.

"No man touches me," Sage snapped.

Reb Jenkins' face twisted in anger, but before he could
press the quarrel, Harley Langford came to the door of his
office and held up an imperious forefinger.

"Reb!" he called.

Harley Langford was fifty, but looked years younger.
He was the biggest man on the ranch, standing six feet
four in his stockinged feet with shoulders in proportion.
He weighed well over two hundred pounds and not an
ounce of it was excess fat. He could do anything any man
on the ranch could do and he could do it better.

Reb Jenkins started for the office, but Sage, walking
faster, passed him. "Dad!" she exclaimed. "I want to
have a talk with you."

"Later, Sage," Harley Langford said. "I've some business to take up with Reb now."

"It can wait," Sage cried. "This is important."

"So's my business," her father replied in annoyance.

"As important as Emmett's life?"

"What's that?"

"I just kept him from being killed."

Harley Langford looked sharply at his daughter, then shot a quick glance at his foreman.

"All right, Reb," he growled.

"He can hear what I've got to say," Sage said. "It concerns him as much as it does the rest of us. The man Emmett was going to fight was the same one who—who shot him." She nodded at Reb.

Reb exclaimed, "You mean he had the nerve to come down from the hills?"

"He was in Meadowlands an hour ago."

"Sage," Harley Langford said impatiently, "you're getting yourself all involved again. Did Emmett have a fight or didn't he?"

"I've been trying to tell you—they were just about to draw and shoot it out when I stopped them."

"How do you mean, you stopped them?"

"Just what I said; I rode in between them and—" Sage winced a little. "Well, I used this." She held up her riding whip.

Langford stared at the whip. "You *what?*"

"I hit them with this. Emmett, as well as the stranger."

Langford cried out. "You struck this—this gun fighter with your whip?"

"Of course. He was taunting Emmett and you know that fool brother of mine. He'll accept a dare from anyone, whether he stands a chance or not."

Langford suddenly grunted. "And this terrible gun fighter turned tail and ran when you beat him with your whip?"

He made an impatient gesture. "I don't think Emmett was in any danger."

"Oh, no?" Sage's lip curled. "You forget what that man did yesterday to Reb . . . and the others."

"I told you we got bushwhacked," Reb Jenkins snarled. "He got the drop on us when we weren't expecting him."

"That isn't what Bill Anson and Hank Butler said."

"Those yellow-livered cowards!" Reb snapped. "I fired them for turning tail yesterday and if they keep on blabbin' they're going to get—"

"What Kirby got?" The words came out before Sage realized what she was saying, but as Reb's eyes glowed she realized that the gibe had been a cruel one. "I'm sorry, Reb; I shouldn't have said that."

"It's all right," Reb grated. "Kirby got it, yes, but I'm not forgettin' it. If it wasn't for this arm I'd be riding into town right now."

"I don't think that will be necessary, Reb," Harley Langford said curtly. "He'll be taken care of. In fact," he hesitated and his eyes went past Sage and Reb, toward the bunkhouses at the far edge of the cottonwoods. He drew a deep breath. "Tell Sloane I want to see him, Reb."

"Sloane!" cried Sage. "That—that murderer!"

Langford stepped back into his office. "Come in, Sage," he said sharply. "You and I are going to have a little talk."

"I think it's time we did," Sage retorted. She followed her father into the office.

Outside, Reb Jenkins glowered at the office door a moment, then turned and headed for the bunkhouses.

In the office, a square room of about twenty by twenty, Harley Langford strode to his desk and seated himself in a great chair.

"Sage," he began, "you're twenty-one years old and you haven't had a spanking in more than ten years—"

"And you're not going to spank me now," Sage said, suddenly calm.

"Maybe not," Harley Langford admitted grimly. "But there are times when it seems that nothing less will hold you in line. Like now."

"Because I stopped Emmett from getting into a gun fight?"

"Emmett can take care of himself. He's handled a gun for a dozen years."

"I know," Sage said. "I've watched him banging away out behind the corrals. And I've seen him taking lessons from that killer, Sloane. Sloane's filed down his trigger and he's taught him how to draw. Emmett does it all nice and fancy. Sloane's showed him how; there's only one thing he hasn't taught him—how to keep the other man from drawing faster!"

Langford was silent a moment. Then he drew a deep breath and shook his head. "Sage," he said slowly, "Emmett isn't my son, but I feel for him exactly what I feel for you."

"I know you do, Dad. And I love Emmett as much as if he *were* my brother. That's why I don't want him killed."

"A man has to take his chances," Langford went on. "He has to fight in this country."

"Now we're getting to the subject I want to talk about. Something's going on around here."

"What?"

"That's what I'm asking *you.*"

"I don't know what you're talking about, Sage."

"I think you do. It's all around. I can feel it here, in Meadowlands—everywhere. We've got more men on the ranch than we've ever had and they're not doing any more work. And this affair yesterday; Reb hasn't told the truth about it."

"You think one man—this stranger—shot up Reb and Kirby and Anson and Butler?"

"I don't know, but I overheard something in town this morning. Something about Ellis . . . and you."

"What did you hear?"

"That there was trouble between you, and that you'd threatened to run him out of the country." Sage paused a moment. "And they say Ellis has disappeared and his house was burned down last night."

Harley Langford suddenly got to his feet and came out from behind his desk. There was a frown of concentration on his face, but it eased away as he came to some decision in his mind. "All right, Sage," he said. "I'm going to tell you. Maybe it's better that you know in case something— well, in case I'm not around."

"You think something *might* happen to you?"

Langford shrugged. "It never has, and it won't this time." He clenched a huge fist. "They think I've lost my grip, but they'll find out I haven't. I'm as good a man as I ever was and when this is all over there'll be just one ranch here, the H-L."

"Then you're fighting the other ranchers!"

"They're fighting me. They think I've got too much range and they're trying to take it away from me."

"Who?"

"Rudabaugh, Allison, Macfadden, and all the other two-bit ranchers like Ellis. It's Langford against the lot of them."

"But there's room enough for all of them, Dad; why should they want to take our range?"

"No man ever has enough land, Sage. If he's got forty acres, he wants eighty and if he's got a half million he wants a million. I've got eighty thousand acres and it so happens that it's the best grass country this side of the mountains. Well, why shouldn't it be? I was the first man here. I fought the Indians and I fought the Mormons. I made the H-L and I'm going to keep it. I'm not going to give up one inch of my range."

A little shudder ran through Sage as she watched her father. This was the Harley Langford of whom she had heard, the man who was tougher than any of his riders. It was the man of whom she had heard, but not the one she knew. That was a different Harley Langford.

She said: "So there's going to be fighting . . . and killing . . ."

Outside the office, boots crunched on hard soil, and Sage, turning, saw Sam Sloane approaching the open doorway. Sloane was a man in his middle thirties, old for a gun fighter. He was about six feet tall, with a slight stoop. He was lean and swarthy, had a hooked nose and wore huge mustaches. His face was oddly reminiscent of that of a vulture.

He stopped just outside the door. "You want to see me, boss?" he asked, slurring his words.

Sage looked at her father, hesitated, then nodding, went through the door. As she walked past him, Sloane's beady eyes studied her closely and he even turned slightly to watch her after, as she walked outside toward the ranch house.

Langford's sharp voice turned him back. "I've got some work for you, Sloane."

"Sure 'nough, boss?" Sloane asked. He entered the office. "Glad to hear it; things been awful quiet and me, I'm a man who likes to keep busy."

"I think you'll soon get your fill of work." Langford looked sourly at the gun fighter a moment, then suddenly said: "Do you know Roy Dorcas, Sloane?"

"You mean have I heard of him? Sure, everybody's heard of Roy Dorcas."

"I didn't say that; I said do you *know* Dorcas?"

Sloane held up his hands, palms upwards. "Now, boss, you been hearin' some wrong things about me. You know how people are, give a dog a bad name—"

Langford interrupted him coldly. "You don't have to

gild yourself for me, Sam Sloane. I know what you are—a killer. I hired you for that reason only, and you know it. So we can forget all that other nonsense. Now do you, or don't you, know Roy Dorcas?"

Sloane said: "Yes."

"All right. Do you know where to find him?"

Sloane bared his teeth. "Now look, Langford, you said right about me a minute ago. There ain't many things I draw the line at, but if you think I'm goin' against Roy Dorcas—"

"Will you hold that tongue of yours a minute?" Langford snarled at the gun fighter. "Nobody's asking you to go gunning for Dorcas. All I want you to do is find Dorcas and tell him I want to see him."

"I can find him, all right, boss. As a matter of fact, I know just about where to look for him and it ain't so far from here, but gettin' him to come here is another thing."

"Dorcas will come," Langford said. "Just tell him I want to see him. He'll come, all right."

Four

——◦•══════•◦——

SHORTLY before five o'clock a little dour-faced man with a scraggy beard pulled out a chair across the table from where Ralls sat playing a game of solitaire.

"You're the man put Kirby Jenkins out of business," he said.

Ralls looked up from his game and gave the little man a quick but thorough examination, then dropped his eyes to his cards and put a black ten on a red jack.

The bearded man grunted. "Don't brag much, do you?"

"Is this Kirby Jenkins something to brag about?" Ralls asked quietly.

"He is, if it's true that his brother, Reb, got winged at the same time and a couple of other H-L men were around." The other man cleared his throat. "I'm Alec Macfadden."

Ralls nodded, but continued to lay out cards. Macfadden exclaimed angrily, "Ain't you got enough politeness to say howdy when a man gives you his name?"

"I don't recall asking you to sit down and talk," Ralls retorted.

Macfadden's mean-looking little eyes glinted as he looked murderously at Ralls, but it was wasted, for Ralls refused to look up from his game of solitaire.

"I was going to offer you a job," Macfadden snarled,

"but if that's the way you're going to act you can go to hell." He kicked back his chair and stamped off toward the bar, where he ordered a glass of whiskey and downed it in a single gulp, an amazing thing for the Scotchman who knew the value of money and sometimes nursed a two-ounce glass of whiskey for an hour.

Ralls played his game to an impasse, then shuffled the cards and played another game, in which he actually got out twenty-two cards before he was compelled to admit defeat.

He gathered up the cards, then, squared them and pushed back his chair. He looked around Cagle's Saloon and discovered that quite a few customers had come into the place. But the gambling games, he noted, were idle. The patrons were all gathered along the bar, where several men were gathered at the street end.

Ralls, starting in that direction, saw eyes suddenly averted and shifted his course and headed for the center of the bar. Les Cagle left the bar and intercepted him.

" 'Bout supper time, isn't it?" he asked.

Ralls looked toward the end of the bar. "Is it?"

Cagle hesitated, then exhaled slightly and stepped to one side. Ralls moved to the bar and signaled to Herman. "Beer."

The man brought the glass of suds and Ralls took hold of the glass and waited for the foam to settle. Along the bar the knot of men opened like a flower and a man came out of the group. He was a big man, although not too big; he stood a little above six feet and weighed in the neighborhood of two hundred pounds. His solid frame was heavily muscled. His face was crisscrossed with little white scars. One ear was mangled and his nose was slightly askew.

He came toward Ralls, his face thrust forward and head cocked to one side. He said: "I'm Ben Rudabaugh, Mister."

"All right," Ralls said shortly, "say your piece."

Rudabaugh grinned wickedly. "I haven't got a gun—I never carry one."

Ralls said bitterly, "I never saw a meaner bunch of people than around this neighborhood. Everybody wants to fight."

"Seems to me you've been doing a little fighting yourself," Rudabaugh said.

Ralls picked up the heavy beer glass by the handle and crashed it over Rudabaugh's head. The big man reeled back, caught himself on the bar and stood there for a moment, wiping beer and blood and glass from his face.

He said: "It's all right, I'm glad you did that. Now I can beat you to a pulp and it won't bother me none afterwards."

"You wanted the fight," Ralls said. He suddenly stepped back and peeled off his coat with a quick tear and shrug. Rudabaugh came forward, walking on the balls of his feet, his hands clenched before him.

A tiny frown creased Ralls' forehead. Rudabaugh was a fighter. The scars on his face indicated that, and they were verified by the fact that he carried no gun in a land where a gun was as essential as a hat. Rudabaugh carried none because he was a fist fighter and wanted all his fights to be decided by brawn alone.

He came toward Ralls now, with his fists raised. Ralls retreated along the bar, which was not lost upon Rudabaugh. The man was afraid of him, even though he had opened the fight with a savage and unfair blow.

Rudabaugh's right flickered out in a quick feint. He followed through with his left. The blow grazed Ralls' shoulder harmlessly as he suddenly stooped halfway to the floor, lunged forward and drove his right fist into Rudabaugh's stomach. The blow stung Ralls' entire arm, for Rudabaugh's stomach was a solid ridge of corded muscle. Rudabaugh went back, yet even as he retreated he chopped down with his right and hit Ralls in the small of the back.

Ralls went down to his knees and Rudabaugh, exclaiming in triumph, leaped forward and smashed Ralls' face with his knee.

Ralls' body jackknifed upward and backward and he crashed to the floor on his back. Only his dire peril saved him then. By all rights, he should have lain on his back for seconds, until he caught his wind again, but instinct told him that Rudabaugh would not give him that time and he called upon his reserves and rolled to his left side, so that Rudabaugh's savage kick missed his head.

Then Ralls' hands darted out, caught the heavy boot as it was being drawn back. He twisted it savagely and Rudabaugh crashed to the floor.

That gave Ralls sufficient time to gain his feet and draw a great breath. Rudabaugh scrambled to his own feet and lunged forward for the knockout, but Ralls retreated. His back touched a table and he sidestepped quickly as Rudabaugh rushed him, swinging with both fists.

One caught Ralls a glancing blow on the forehead and Ralls thought that a sledgehammer had struck him. He leaped back, but at that Rudabaugh was the master. He stepped in quickly, drove a terrific blow to Ralls' stomach and as he bent forward, gasping, straightened him with an uppercut that registered down to Ralls' heels.

A roaring filled Ralls' ears. He was gasping for breath and fire seemed to sear his lungs. He saw his opponent through a haze that seemed to magnify him into a giant. He saw a huge fist sizzling toward him and chopped down frantically on it with his right and as it struck, with his left. It, too, collided with the arm and Ralls opened his fists and clung to the arm with his hands.

Rudabaugh jerked back to free his arm and pulled Ralls with him. Ralls fell against his bigger opponent and buried his face in Rudabaugh's chest.

Rudabaugh tried to shake him off but Ralls clung for his life.

"Let go," panted Rudabaugh, "let go, or by God . . ."

He planted his free hand against the side of Ralls' face, shoved furiously. Ralls held his grip for another second. The brief respite was clearing his head and suddenly he let go of Rudabaugh, rather he let the big man push him away.

And then as he went back, he struck at Rudabaugh, a hard blow again, into the corded stomach, then another and another. He shot a quick glance into Rudabaugh's face, saw that it was twisted in rage. But it seemed to Ralls that the expression was the least bit strained.

He sidestepped a stinging blow that Rudabaugh should have landed. It was a split second slow and Ralls, sensing that Rudabaugh was tiring, feinted with his left, ducked and sidestepped at the same time. He crashed a hard right through Rudabaugh's guard and landed on the other man's face. He followed with a left to the same spot, took a crashing blow on the side of his face and, leaping in, clinched with Rudabaugh.

The fighter was stronger than Ralls and wrestled him clear, but Ralls, again allowing himself to be shoved back, struck at the stomach once more.

He shot another look into Rudabaugh's face and now he was sure that the twisted expression was frozen. He moved to the left and Rudabaugh followed.

He feinted and jumped back without a blow. Rudabaugh followed and did not even try to block the feint that Ralls tried again. He was closing in for the kill, was willing to take a blow or two to land one. Ralls' back touched a table and he reached behind him swiftly and gripping the table with both hands, whirled it around and shoved it at Rudabaugh. The big man stumbled over it, fell to one knee, but came up quickly—to take a blow in his face.

His nose was bleeding now and he shook his head so that drops of blood spattered on Ralls.

"Stand still!" he cried.

"I'm standing," said Ralls. And he did stand for a moment. Rudabaugh came in, his right fist cocked. Ralls smashed him in the midriff with everything he had. Rudabaugh's cocked fist sizzled forward and exploded on Ralls' jaw and Ralls went reeling back.

He staggered back a good six feet and would have fallen except that the bar brought him up. He stood against it a moment, quivering and utterly weary.

Rudabaugh advanced on him. Ralls lowered his head, braced his shoulders against the top of the bar and using it as a lever went out to meet Rudabaugh.

He met Rudabaugh with a weak blow to his chin, drove his other fist again into the stomach, hit Rudabaugh in the face, then once more in the stomach—and took a pile-driving blow on his jaw and neck.

He went down to his knees, with his back touching the bar and Rudabaugh could have finished him then. But Rudabaugh stood over him, his feet planted wide apart, his mouth open and gasping for air. He stood there with his fists raised, ready to fight, but he could fight no longer.

Ralls came up, struck at Rudabaugh's face, then again into that muscular stomach. Only this time it wasn't muscular. It was weak and flabby and Ralls' fist went in three inches.

A groan of agony came from Rudabaugh's throat. He still stood on his feet, but only his giant heart kept him there. He was out but refused to admit it.

Ralls drew back his fist for a last blow, but instead opened his hand and, placing it on Rudabaugh's chest, pushed hard. Rudabaugh swayed like a giant oak tree—and crashed to the floor. He rolled over on his stomach and lay still, except for a few twitching muscles.

For a moment Ralls stared down at his fallen opponent.

Somewhere a voice said: "You've beaten him."

Then Ralls shook his head and nausea swept through him. He shuddered and reeled aside. A hand took his arm, a strong firm hand that led him to a door and into a room and helped him to sit down on a cot. Ralls let go then and dropped to his back. Hands lifted up his feet and deposited them on the cot.

Ralls closed his eyes and let his outraged body take possession of him. He drew huge breaths of air, exhaled them. And after awhile he slept.

Five

RALLS woke up once and was aware that a light was shining in his eyes and that someone was moving about in the room. He forced his eyes open and after awhile was able to focus them on a roll-top desk at which a man was seated. The man looked vaguely familiar but Ralls was too weary to put his brain to the task of recognizing him. He let his eyes go shut and he slept some more.

The next time he opened his eyes the sun was shining on his face. He had more than slept the clock around. He sat up, swinging his booted feet to the floor and was suddenly aware of agonizing pains in various parts of his body. His head ached. He touched his face and discovered three or four bruised, swollen spots.

He drew a deep breath, wincing, then got heavily to his feet and looked around the room. It was about twelve by fourteen and contained besides the cot on which Ralls had slept, the roll-top desk, an iron safe and a couple of chairs.

Ralls stepped to the door and opened it, looking into the barroom where he had fought Ben Rudabaugh. It was deserted except for a swamper who was sloshing down the floor with bucketsful of water and a bartender, polishing glasses. Both men looked curiously at Ralls, but did not speak to him, and he went through the place, out upon the street.

There he discovered that his two horses were both still hitched to the rail, having stood there since the afternoon before without water or feed. Whoever had taken care of Ralls had neglected his horses.

Ralls untied the animals and led them up the street to a livery stable where he arranged for their care.

Leaving the stable, he looked down the street and saw a weathered sign, reading: *Ella's Cafe.* He walked to the restaurant and entered. It was a long, narrow room containing a counter, with stools and a half dozen tables. There was only one customer in it, an elderly, whiskered man who sat on a stool at the end of the counter nearest the kitchen.

Ralls straddled a stool at the front and a girl came from the kitchen. She was in her middle twenties, a clear-eyed, fresh-faced girl in a crisp white uniform.

"Good morning," she said cheerfully, to Ralls.

Ralls nodded acknowledgment. "Good morning. I'd like something to eat."

"Believe it or not," the girl said, "that's what I sell here, food and nothing but food."

"You're Ella?"

"Ella Snow, at your service. With hot cakes and sausage, eggs and ham, coffee."

"All right, I'll have them."

"Hot cakes or . . . ?"

"All of them."

"Guess fighting makes a man hungry."

Ralls looked at her sharply, then realized that his face showed the marks of combat.

"You should have seen the other fellow," Ella went on. "He was in here last night."

"Rudabaugh?" Ralls shook his head. "He made a quicker recovery than I did—and I thought I won."

"Oh, you did, all right. Everybody in town's talking about it."

She stopped as the door opened and Les Cagle came in. The saloonkeeper came forward.

"Have a good sleep?" he asked, then without waiting for a reply he said to Ella Snow, "Ella, you get more beautiful every day."

"And you get richer every day," Ella retorted.

Cagle seated himself on a stool beside Ralls. "Not rich enough."

The girl went off to the kitchen and Cagle looked sideways at Ralls. "You can fight a bit. That was the first time in his life Rudabaugh ever took a beating."

"It'll probably be the last, because I'm not going to fight him again," Ralls said.

"I wouldn't say there was much future in it."

Ralls shook his head. "Thanks for the use of your bed."

"It's all right. I was going out to the ranch, anyway." He hesitated. "That's what I want to talk to you about."

"The ranch?"

"I'd like you to work for me."

"Why?"

"Because I can use a good man."

"Everybody around here seems to want a man," Ralls said. "A fighting man."

Cagle looked sharply at Ralls. "Who else?"

"Little man with whiskers. Said his name was Macfadden."

Cagle looked down at the counter. Ella brought two cups of coffee and set them before the men and went off again to the kitchen. Cagle put milk into his coffee, stirred in some sugar, then said:

"Yes, a fighting man can just about name his own salary these days."

"Range war?"

"I guess you could call it that. Langford against the rest of us. Or you might say the valley against Langford. But don't get the idea that that's a one-sided fight. Langford's a curly wolf and he's got some pretty rough people working for him. That's why I'm glad you had that fight with the Jenkins boys—and young Langford. Means you won't be on their side."

"Whose side is Rudabaugh on?"

Cagle hesitated. "As a matter of fact, he's with us. You might even say he's our leader. Leastwise he's got the biggest spread outside of Langford's."

"Who else is on your side?"

"The little Scotchman you mentioned, Macfadden, and Allison, and—well, a half dozen small chaps like me. There was a man named Ellis, but something seems to have happened to him."

"Something happened to him, all right," Ralls said. "He went over the mountain. . . ."

"What do you mean?"

"Ellis was the cause of the trouble I had with the Jenkins boys; they were going to hang him and I stopped it."

"You faced four men just to save Ellis?"

"If I hadn't, Ellis would have stretched rope."

Cagle frowned. "And Ellis lit out after you saved his life?"

"I guess he figured the law wouldn't be of much help."

Cagle grunted. "You've talked to the sheriff."

"I talked to a man who wore a star."

"That's what I meant. It takes more than a star to make a sheriff. Well, what about it?"

Ralls shook his head slowly. "I don't know the right or the wrong of it, Cagle, but I don't think I'll sit in—on either side."

Cagle's face showed disappointment. "You'll be riding on, then?"

"Not yet." He looked at Cagle. "Any reason I should?"

"It's hard to be neutral in a war—when the bullets are coming at you from both directions."

Ella Snow came from the kitchen, carrying a trayful of food, most of which she set down before Ralls. Cagle received only two slices of toast.

Ella went off and Ralls was eating when Cagle said: "You know, you haven't told me your name."

"That's right, I haven't." Ralls ate another mouthful of food, then said, "It's Ralls."

Beside him Cagle suddenly stiffened. "*Jim Ralls!*"

"Yes."

Cagle was staring at Ralls in astonishment. "No wonder you licked the Jenkins boys." He shook his head. "And you fought Ben Rudabaugh with your fists." He leaned toward Ralls. "Ralls, stay here, work for me just a month. I'll make it worth your while."

"I never worked for a man but once in my life," Ralls said. "And that was Uncle Sam."

"The war?"

Ralls nodded. "And I don't think I'll work for anyone else, until I finish a little job of my own." He paused. "I'm looking for a man."

"Here?"

"I don't know. I think so."

"What's his name? I know just about everybody in the valley."

"The name is . . . Rance Martindale."

The name seemed to make no impression on Cagle. "I don't think there's anyone by that name around here."

"Oh, he's using a different name."

"Well, what does he look like?"

"I don't know."

"You mean you've never seen him?"

"No."

"Then all you've got to go by is a name." Cagle

squinted as his eyes searched Ralls' face. "What makes you think your man is here?"

"Because I've looked everywhere else."

Cagle exclaimed, "I've heard of you, Jim Ralls. So, I guess, has everybody in the West. A lot of people don't even believe you exist. You're a legend. You're in Texas today, in Kansas tomorrow, in Montana the next day. You've been in the gold camps and the cattle towns and you followed the Union Pacific across the plains. You've had a lot of fights and people say you're the fastest man with a gun in the West. You've left a trail of dead men behind you. Personally, I always took those stories with a grain of salt, but what I've seen and heard of you since yesterday has changed my mind. I think the stories are true. In fact, I don't think they've told half enough."

Ralls looked bleakly at his food. "A man gets a reputation," he said, "and there are fools who make you back it up. Like Rudabaugh last night. Only mostly they want to fight with guns. Anybody who's ever hit a tin can with a bullet fancies himself a shot. Yes, I've had to fight—I've had to fight to live. But there's only one fight I've ever looked for . . ."

"Rance Martindale?"

"Rance Martindale. When I've had that fight—if I win—I take off my guns. For keeps."

"Does Martindale know you're looking for him?"

"He knows *somebody's* looking for him."

"But he doesn't know it's you?"

"I think he does."

Cagle's forehead furrowed in thought. "How long have you been hunting for—for Martindale?"

"Quite awhile."

Cagle flushed. "I wasn't trying to pry, Ralls. I thought the length of time might—well, might help narrow your search. I've been here since '68 and I know everybody who's settled here since that time."

"I was looking for him before '68," Ralls said.

Cagle finished his coffee and drummed his fingertips on the counter for a moment. Then he put down a coin and got to his feet.

"I'll see you, Ralls."

Ralls hesitated. He was on the verge of asking the saloonkeeper to keep his identity a secret, but decided against it. Broadcasting his name in the vicinity might serve to smoke out Rance Martindale.

Cagle went out and Ralls finished his breakfast. Ella Snow came out of the kitchen as he was putting down his fork.

"How much?" Ralls asked.

"This one's on the house."

Ralls looked at her in surprise.

"For free, mister," Ella Snow said. "By way of welcoming a newcomer to town." And as Ralls still looked at her sharply: "Or maybe for giving Ben Rudabaugh the licking he's deserved for a long time."

Ralls shook his head. "Whipping Rudabaugh was my own pleasure."

"Then let's say it's for taking me to the peace powwow tonight."

"What peace powwow?"

"Oh, didn't Cagle tell you? The ranchers are having a dance. To get them in the proper mood to talk things over . . . or, to have a last fling before the war. Take your choice."

"I'm sorry, but I don't think I'll be attending." Ralls took a silver dollar from his pocket and laid it on the counter. The girl flushed at his rebuff.

He walked stiffly to the door. With his hand on the knob he stopped and was half inclined to go back and pick up the dollar, but Ella Snow said: "Thank you, sir," and he went out of the restaurant, swearing softly to himself.

Six

———◆◆◆———

HIS horses had been fed, watered and curry-combed. Paying the liveryman, Ralls saddled up and rode out, the pack horse trailing behind. Two or three men watched him as he rode down the street headed in the direction of Langford's horseshoe-shaped valley.

He was passing the last house on the street when he heard the pounding of horse's hoofs. Turning in the saddle, he saw a rider bearing down on him.

He was a young, redheaded chap mounted on a tough cow pony. He went past Ralls at a full gallop and did not even look at him. It seemed to Ralls, in fact, that he deliberately averted his eyes as he went by.

A messenger, Ralls thought. It didn't matter, for Ralls was already on the alert. He had to be to live. Yet, a half mile from Meadowlands he left the traveled highway and cut across the range. He rode for a half hour, through grass that came to his horses' knees, rich green grass that indicated good soil and plenty of rain.

A range that cattlemen dreamed about.

He saw plenty of cattle, fat beeves that were ready for market. But nowhere did he see riders. Not until he crossed a little stream and skirted a clump of cottonwoods.

Then a man rode out from among the trees. A rifle was

41

across his pommel and he wore a revolver at his hip. He regarded Ralls sullenly and would have passed without speaking, except that Ralls hailed him.

"This the way to the Langford Ranch?"

The man threw a curt "yes" at Ralls and continued without pulling up his horse, but Ralls made note of the fact that he altered his horse so that he was riding side-wards to Ralls and could observe him until he rode out of gunshot range.

A little while later he spied a clump of ranch buildings in a tree-studded hollow, but decided that the buildings were not large enough for the H-L Ranch and gave them a wide berth.

Beyond the ranch he passed a pair of cowboys who nodded and spoke the time of the day, but continued about their business, which was unlike cowboys. Ralls sighed lightly. There was trouble brewing on this range, all right.

Ahead was a sizable herd of Herefords and riding close Ralls noted the H-L brand. A short distance beyond was another good herd of Herefords and from then on the range was dotted with H-L cattle.

Topping a rise he saw below a well-traveled trail and crossed to it. He followed it for a mile until it swung to the left and ran up an easy grade to a grassy hill. From the summit Ralls looked down upon the headquarters of the H-L. It could be no other from the size and number of the buildings.

A rider who came jogging along confirmed Ralls' opinion. Ralls rode down the hill, following the road into the ranch yard. There was considerable activity at the corrals, he noted, as he rode up, but no one came forward until he reached the office building and was dismounting.

Then Harley Langford stepped out. He stopped when he saw Ralls.

"Lookin' for me?" he demanded.

"If you're Harley Langford, yes."

"I am. But I'm not hiring, although you can get a meal if you go around to the cook shack."

"Thanks; but I've had my breakfast."

"Then what do you want?"

"Why, I just thought I'd drop around and see your place."

Langford looked at Ralls suspiciously. "You wouldn't by any chance be the stranger who picked a fight with my son yesterday?" He shook his head. "Of course not. He wouldn't have the nerve to ride up here."

"Well," said Ralls, "I'm a stranger in these parts and I did have some words with your son, but if he said *I* picked the fight he didn't tell the truth of it."

Harley Langford took a couple of quick steps forward. "But you're the man who killed Kirby Jenkins and winged Reb . . . !" His hand went automatically to the gun at his thigh, but as the hand closed over the butt of the weapon Ralls called out to him:

"Hold it, Langford!"

Langford's hand froze on his gun butt. "You got a nerve comin' here . . ."

"All right," said Ralls, "I shot it out with the Jenkinses, but did they tell you what they were doing at the time?"

"I don't give a good goddam what they were doing," Langford snapped. "They were my riders and the H-L fights for its own. Right or wrong. Get that, right or wrong."

"Even if they were hanging a man?"

"Ellis wasn't a man—he was a skunk!"

"He deserved killing?"

"He was a rustler and in this country we hang rustlers."

"I thought there was a law that took care of things like that."

Langford's features twisted. "I was here before there was a law and I can still take care of my own fights." He shot a quick look in the direction of the corrals. "But come to think of it, it ain't fair for me to shoot it out with you. Reb's Kirby's brother. He's got a better claim on you than I have.''

"I don't think Reb'll take that claim."

"The hell he won't," Langford sneered. "Just because you got the drop on him . . .''

"Why don't you call Reb?"

"I will." Langford looked again toward the corrals, but he did not call for his foreman. He looked sharply at Ralls. "Pretty sure of yourself."

"No," said Ralls, "I'm not sure of myself at all. But I've got a job to do and I mean to do it." He paused a moment. "I'm looking for a man. I understand you've been around here as long as anybody. I thought maybe you might know this man.''

Something seemed to go out of Harley Langford, then. He looked steadily at Ralls. "What's his name?"

"Rance Martindale."

He was braced, Ralls knew, and yet a little shiver seemed to run through Langford. The end of the trail was in sight and Ralls leaned forward in his saddle, so he would not miss the slightest change of expression in Langford's face.

Langford knew!

But Langford said: "Never heard the name."

"You're sure?"

"Of course I'm sure," Langford snapped. "I was the first white man in this section. I've watched all the others come in and I've never heard of a man named—what was it?—Martingale?''

"Martindale," corrected Ralls. And if he had been sure before, he was doubly sure now. Langford had overdone it. He knew, all right.

"Martindale," repeated Langford musingly. "Not exactly a name you'd forget, is it?"

"No," said Ralls. "Especially if you've got reason to remember it."

"And you have? What'd you say your name was?"

"It doesn't matter, if you don't know anyone named Martindale." Ralls picked up his reins. "Thanks."

He turned his horse and started away from Langford. And Langford let him go. Which was in itself an admission, for had Langford not been violently upset he would never have permitted Ralls to ride off.

Langford remained in front of his office door, watching Ralls ride away. When Ralls was a hundred feet away he was still standing there. And then Sage came around the corner of the building and saw her father. "Who was that, Dad?" she asked.

Langford was not even aware of his daughter's presence. She repeated her question. "Who was that, Dad?"

Then Langford shook himself. "Oh—hello, Sage. I don't know, he didn't give his name."

"He looks like the man I—I struck yesterday," Sage said. "But of course he wouldn't . . ."

"Yes," Langford said suddenly. "That's the man."

Sage exclaimed, "He came out *here?*"

"You see him, don't you?" Langford said irascibly.

"Yes, I see him," said Sage. "I see him riding away from the H-L—after he killed one of its riders and wounded another." Sage looked squarely into her father's face. "And I see a ghost in your eyes, Dad! What did he say to you? Who is he?"

"I don't know," Langford said dully. "Maybe—maybe *he's* a ghost. I don't know."

His shoulders slumped, Langford walked past his daughter in the direction of the house.

Seven

THE dance was being held in the Meadowlands town hall and a spirit of gaiety prevailed that was not shared by the ranchers who met next door in the office of Judge Gordon. There were ten or twelve men in the room, all ranchers with the exception of Judge Gordon and Sheriff Cherry; that was counting Cagle, the saloonkeeper, as a rancher.

Judge Gordon was doing his best to preside over the meeting but was finding the role of peacemaker a thankless one, for none of the men present had come to the meeting with an open mind.

Ben Rudabaugh expressed the consensus of opinion of the smaller ranchers. "All this talk of respect for one another's boundary lines is a lot of hogwash and you know it. We're squabbling for one reason only—Horseshoe Valley."

"Which is mine," Harley Langford snarled.

"By what right?" Rudabaugh demanded. "Do you own the land? Did you ever buy it?"

"Did you buy *your* land?" Langford retorted.

"No," Rudabaugh admitted, "I didn't. The land was here and I settled on it—like everybody else."

"Ane I settled in Horseshoe Valley."

46

"On eighty thousand acres. Which is as much as all the rest of us put together have got."

Alec Macfadden jumped up from his chair. "You got no right to all that land, Harley Langford."

"I've got as much right to it as you have to your land."

"You haven't got a right to eighty thousand acres, when I've only got six."

"There's ten million acres of land west of you. Help yourself to as much of it as you want."

"That's desert land, not fit for cattle raising."

Langford glowered at Macfadden. "So it isn't just land you want, it's *my* land."

"You've hogged all the worthwhile land and you know it," Ben Rudabaugh shouted.

"I was here first," replied Langford. "Sure. I took up the best land; why shouldn't I have? In a gold strike the discoverer takes the best claim, doesn't he? I found Horseshoe Valley and I took it. I had to fight Indians to hold it. And by God, I'll fight anyone who tries to take it away from me." He leaped to his feet and circled the group with a pointing index finger. "And that goes for you and you and you!"

"You'll get your fight!" Rudabaugh cried. "You'll get it right now." He started toward Langford, but the latter fixed him with a cold eye.

"Lay a hand on me, Ben Rudabaugh," he said, "and I'll pistol whip you." He sneered. "Looks like you didn't get enough of fighting yesterday."

Rudabaugh was quite conscious of his battered features. His face twitched angrily. "Maybe I owe you for that."

"What are you talking about?"

"You've been hiring some mighty peculiar people lately. Sam Sloane—this stranger, who picked the fight with me."

Langford looked narrowly at Rudabaugh. "Are you crazy? The stranger killed Kirby Jenkins and wounded Reb."

"At least that's your story."

Langford whirled on the sheriff. "Cherry, pick him up. Throw him in your hoosegow and see if I make one move to do anything for him."

The sheriff winced. His eyes shot to the face of Cagle, the saloonkeeper, but the latter returned his glance impassively. Until the sheriff looked away and then a faint, derisive grin cracked his features.

The sheriff cleared his throat a couple of times. "Well, I dunno's I can properly arrest him . . ."

"Why not? You're sheriff of this county, aren't you?"

"Y-yes," admitted the sheriff, "but somebody's got to swear out a warrant . . ."

"I'll swear it out."

Cagle appealed to the judge. "That all right?"

"Certainly."

Cherry still looked unhappy. "All right," he finally said, "I'll arrest him."

Jim Ralls came into Meadowlands after nightfall, after riding the range of Horseshoe Valley most of the day. He left his horses at the livery stable and proceeded to Ella Snow's restaurant, where he found the place presided over by a Chinese cook. He ate his dinner, then crossed the street to Cagle's Saloon, which he found so crowded he had to elbow his way to the bar.

Once at the bar he suddenly had plenty of elbow room, however, for the man next to him recognized him and soon the whisper was running along the bar.

The bartender caught Ralls' eye and came over.

"Beer," Ralls said.

The man brought it and Ralls sipped it. He turned away from the bar and was looking at the batwing doors of the place when they bellied inward and Sheriff Cherry entered. He stopped inside the room, searched the crowd and his face fell when he spied Ralls at the bar. He came forward.

"I'm sorry," he said awkwardly, to Ralls. "But I've got a warrant for your arrest."

"Not tonight," Ralls said.

The sheriff blinked. "Huh?"

"Some other time."

"I—uh, you don't understand, stranger. I—I've got to put you under arrest."

Ralls regarded the man steadily. "On what charge?"

"The murder of Kirby Jenkins."

"That's *your* idea?"

"Uh, no," gulped the sheriff. "Harley Langford swore out the warrant."

"Then why don't you get him to serve it?"

"Because I'm the sheriff; that's my job. Uh, this warrant was issued by Judge Gordon." He waited a moment, then a hundred eyes in the room lashed him on. "You've got to come with me."

"No," said Ralls.

A film of perspiration bathed the sheriff's unhappy face. "It ain't a matter of wanting to come. You've *got* to come."

Ralls made a little shooing gesture with the glass of beer in his hand. "Go away."

Along the bar a cowboy said raucously: "Go ahead, Sheriff, take away his gun."

Goaded, the sheriff took a step forward. "Give me your gun, or . . ." He reached for the gun in his own holster.

While the rest of his body remained absolutely still, Ralls' right hand made a flicking movement and the beer from his glass cascaded into the sheriff's face.

The sheriff cried out and leaped back. He collided with a man seated at a table and ricocheted from him—aided by a push—to the floor.

He scrambled to his feet, wiping beer from his face.

"You can't do that to me," he howled.

"It's illegal!" jeered a man at the bar.

The sheriff picked out the man and pointed at him. "You, Tod Meacham, I hereby deputize you to help me in arresting a criminal."

"Deputize, hell!"

"I can do that, Meacham," the sheriff said doggedly. "I can deputize anyone I want and you've got to help me, or go to jail yourself."

"Who's going to arrest *me?*" the man named Meacham asked.

"I am," said a voice at the door.

Judge Gordon came forward, his face dark with anger. "If the sheriff doesn't arrest you," he said to Meacham, "I will."

The unexpected ally gave the sheriff sudden confidence. He pointed at another man. "And you, Milo Hanson, I also deputize you." Then he pointed at still another man. "And you, Dave Lawrence."

He turned on Ralls. "All right, Mister, I call on you now for the last time. Surrender, or . . ."

He squared off significantly.

Ralls set his empty glass upon the bar. The men behind him suddenly scrambled clear and Ralls found that he had plenty of room. He moved a little away from the bar.

"Sheriff," he said, "I'm not surrendering to you or anyone else."

A hushed silence fell upon the room. The sheriff had made his play. He had three deputies and a judge to back him up. He had to go through with the arrest. But the stranger had defied him. There was only one answer now. Gunplay.

Then the silence was broken by a cry from halfway across the room.

"It's Jim Ralls!"

The sheriff flinched as if he had been struck in the face with a fist. "You—you're Jim Ralls?" he croaked.

"Yes!" snapped Ralls.

Sheriff Cherry's deputies suddenly began to back away. "Jim Ralls," one of them said thickly. "I want no part of this."

"Come ahead," Ralls challenged. "If you want to arrest me, draw your guns."

The sheriff sent a wild glance at his retreating deputies, then his eyes went back to Ralls. "No, no," he cried in panic.

Judge Gordon, his face taut, moved forward. "You're really Jim Ralls?" he asked.

"I am," Ralls declared. "And if you've got a charge against me, I'll appear in your court, but I'll be damned if I'll let any two-bit sheriff drag me down to a jail."

The judge swallowed hard. "I'll expect you in court."

He turned on his heel and walked out of the saloon. The deputized deputies scurried out after him. Ralls looked deliberately at the sheriff.

He said: "I'll be around if you decide that you really want me."

And with that he walked past the sheriff toward the door.

The sheriff could have drawn his gun then; he could have shot Jim Ralls in the back. But he didn't. His trigger finger was palsied.

Ralls went through the door.

Eight

———••◆••———

THE hall where the dance was being held was a low one-story building. The double front door was open and the dancers could be seen inside. There were more than fifty people in the hall but only four or five couples were actually dancing. The others were standing about in small, silent groups. The spirit of gaiety that should have prevailed was oddly missing.

Outside the building another dozen or so men stood about, talking in low tones.

Jim Ralls came along the wooden sidewalk and stopped near the door. He looked inside, started to pass, then suddenly wheeled and entered the hall.

Inside, he discovered that a small table had been set up just within the door. An elderly man sat behind it. "Your gun, mister," he said.

Ralls looked at the wall behind the little table and saw a double row of guns hanging from nails. He took out his gun and tendered it to the attendant, butt first.

"Name?"

"Ralls."

The name made no impression on the man. He wrote it on a small tag and tied it to the trigger guard. Ralls moved on into the dance hall proper.

At the far side of the room a four-piece orchestra came to a wheezing finale. The dancers on the floor separated and Ralls saw that one of them was Ella Snow.

She saw him at the same time and came toward him. "So you came, after all."

"Yes," Ralls said. "I stopped by the restaurant, but you'd already left." He hesitated. "Sorry about this morning."

"Oh, it's all right." Her eyes searched his face. "People have been coming into the restaurant all day, talking about you. As a matter of fact I've been doing a lot of thinking about you myself."

Before Ralls could reply to that the orchestra struck up. Ella smiled up at him.

"I'm sorry," Ralls said, "I haven't danced since—"

"Then this is a good time to brush up," Ella said. She held up her hands.

Ralls groaned inwardly as he placed his right hand on the small of her back. They moved off, Ella lightly and Ralls awkwardly attempting to lead her.

It was ten years since Ralls had danced; that had been in Virginia the time he and Tom Sutherland had attended the Rebel ball that a few Southern people had held in defiance of Sheridan, who had taken the town the day before.

The Southern ladies had been pretty cool to them—until Sutherland had won them over. Sutherland had been like that.

Ten long years, during which time Captain Ralls of the Fouth Michigan Cavalry had become Jim Ralls the notorious gun fighter and killer.

Ella Snow was talking. "She dresses and rides like a man and then she can come to a dance and look like that . . ."

Ralls shot a quick look into Ella's face, saw that her eyes were focused on someone over his shoulder. He swiveled his head and looked into the eyes of Sage Langford.

She was dancing with Reb Jenkins whose left arm was in a black silken sling.

She was wearing a dark velvet evening gown and her taffy-colored hair was piled high on the back of her head. Ralls inhaled softly. She was the most beautiful woman he had ever seen. Beside her Ella Snow, in her gingham dress, was a drab farm girl.

Sage's eyes bored into his own. Reb Jenkins turned her away and his own eyes met Ralls'. He scowled and stopped dancing.

"Thought you'd be over the mountain by now," he said, baring his teeth.

"Why, no," Ralls replied. "I'm figuring on staying here in the valley for awhile."

Reb raised the slinged arm. "This'll be better soon."

"You're not left-handed, are you?" Ralls asked, and felt Ella press his hand. He said to her: "Sorry."

"This is a dance, mister." She cocked her head to one side. "By the way, how long do we keep up the mister business?"

"It stops right now," Ralls said. His eyes were on the door, where several men were just entering. Among them were Sheriff Cherry, Ben Rudabaugh, Judge Gordon and Harley Langford.

The group spotted Ralls and began whispering among themselves.

"My name," Ralls said to Ella Snow, "is Jim Ralls."

He could feel her gasp. "Jim Ralls, the—"

"Yes." He took a couple of steps with her, then relaxed his hold. "And now you can stop dancing with me."

"Why?" Ella asked. "Because you've got hydrophobia?"

"Because I'm Jim Ralls."

"And who do you think I thought you were? A sky pilot come to save the souls of our local citizens?" She laughed shortly. "I knew you'd fought Kirby and Reb Jenkins, and I knew you'd beaten Ben Rudabaugh to a pulp. All right, I didn't know you were Jim Ralls. But I did think you might be—well, Roy Dorcas, or one of his men.''

"It didn't make any difference to you?"

"Why should it? I'm an outlaw myself. Sure, people come to eat at my restaurant. Men. But have you seen any of the ranchers' wives waving at me? Did you hear Sage Langford talking to me a minute ago?"

"It's like that, eh?" Ralls remarked.

Then the music stopped and Ella Snow stepped back from him. "Thanks," she said. "Thanks for dancing with me." She walked off.

Ralls was about to follow her, when he saw Ben Rudabaugh coming toward him.

He waited for the big rancher to come up. There was no enmity in the man's face. Only a sardonic humor.

"Hello, Ralls," he said. "Nice fight, wasn't it?"

"So nice that I'm not going to repeat it."

Rudabaugh grinned. "I was hoping you might want to try it again, sometime before I've drunk a gallon of beer." He rubbed his stomach. "I'm not alibiing, you licked me fair and square. But I still would like to try it again."

"No," Ralls said. "I'm satisfied."

Rudabaugh chuckled. "I hear you just about gave the sheriff heart failure."

"I can't help it if he's got a chicken heart."

"Oh, he's got that, all right. But he did shoot a man once. In the back. Just thought I'd mention it." He suddenly changed the subject. "Got anything special in mind, Ralls?"

"Such as what?"

"From what I've heard of you, you don't stay long in one place."

"I plan to stay here awhile." Ralls searched the big cattleman's face. "Didn't Cagle tell you?"

"Cagle? Does he know?" Rudabaugh frowned. "I suppose it's all right, though, if you and Cagle made a deal."

"I've made no deal with Cagle—or anyone."

"You're not on our side, then?"

"I'm on my own side."

Rudabaugh shook his head. "There are only two sides here. Ours and Langford's."

Ralls, looking past Rudabaugh, saw Harley Langford and his daughter talking together animatedly. Langford's face wore a scowl as he talked earnestly, but Sage kept shaking her head.

Ralls turned back to Rudabaugh. "Excuse me." He walked away from the rancher.

Sage, facing him, saw him approach. For a moment her eyes widened, then they glinted.

"I wonder," Ralls said, "if I could have the next dance?"

Langford, whirling, stared at him in astonishment. "Ralls!" he said thickly. Then his face twisted in sudden rage. "You . . . how dare you talk to my daughter . . . !"

Sage said quickly: "Why, yes, Mr. Ralls, I'd love to."

At that moment the music started and Sage held up her hands. Ralls put his arm about her and started to move off.

Langford said savagely: "Sage . . ."

But his daughter gave him a mocking smile.

Ralls and the girl moved out upon the floor. The moment they were sufficiently far away from Harley Langford, Sage looked up at Ralls, her eyes hard. "I was in the middle of an argument with my father when you came up. That's the only reason I'm dancing with you."

"Why," said Ralls, "we can stop if you wish."

"So you're Jim Ralls," she said with unconcealed contempt. "The notorious gun fighter and killer. And I came here tonight, half hoping you would be here, so I could apologize for yesterday."

"That's all right. I accept the intention."

"I'm *not* apologizing," Sage said furiously. "You *were* taunting my brother into a fight. You killers have to feed your ego every now and then, and the only way you can do that is to kill someone.''

"You seem to know quite a lot about killers.''

"We've got one out on the ranch—Sam Sloane. You may meet him one day. I think you'll find him more of a match than my brother.''

"I don't doubt it. I've heard of Sloane.''

"I've heard of you—but nothing good!''

Sage suddenly disengaged her hand from Ralls', and stepped away from him. Ralls saw that there was only one other couple on the floor. He also noted that most of the people in the hall were heading toward the door. Leaving, although it couldn't be more than nine o'clock.

He stood for a moment in the middle of the floor, looking after Sage. He saw her join her father, saw her get a Spanish shawl from a chair where she had evidently deposited it earlier, throw it about her shoulders and start for the door.

Ralls drew a deep breath, exhaled, then followed. As he neared the table where the attendant was returning the checked guns to their owners, a passage was quickly made for him. One woman, whose elbow he happened to touch, gasped and shrank away from him.

The gun attendant looked inquiringly at him.

"Ralls.''

"Ra . . .'' the man began, then winced. "Yes sir, Jim Ralls!'' He found Ralls' gun, tore off the tag and handed it to Ralls.

Ralls holstered the gun and again found a path cleared for him to the door. He went out.

Nine

━━━◆━━━◆━━━

HARLEY LANGFORD had a buckboard, but used it only for special occasions, such as tonight, when he escorted his daughter to Meadowlands and she wore garb unsuitable for riding. But he had little patience with the team that drew the buckboard and he kept urging the horses along.

Perhaps it was just as well, for he was in no mood to carry on a conversation with Sage.

Sage could stand only so much silence, however, and after they had traveled about two miles from Meadowlands, she finally exclaimed: "All right, let's get it over."

"Get what over?" Harley Langford demanded.

"The quarrel. I don't want to stay up half the night . . ."

"I'm not going to keep you up," Harley retorted. "And I'm not going to quarrel with you."

"I'd rather have a fight than see you sulk."

"Stop it, Sage. Of course I didn't want you to dance with a man like Ralls. But it isn't that . . ."

"What is it, then?"

Langford shook his head. "Didn't you see that crowd leave the dance when it was less than an hour old?"

"Yes, but I thought that was because of—well, because the gunman was there."

Langford grunted. "Ralls is one gun fighter more or less. They left tonight when *I* came in."

"I don't understand."

"Of course you don't. We had a meeting tonight." Langford paused a moment. "I told you yesterday what was brewing. Well, it isn't brewing any more. It's boiling now."

Sage exclaimed, "You mean there'll be . . . fighting?"

"There'll be fighting."

Sage exclaimed, "Isn't there any chance to—to compromise?"

"I wouldn't compromise if I could," Langford cried. "I'll fight them to the bitter end. And I'll beat them. When it's over this will all be H-L land."

Ahead of the buckboard a hundred yards, a horse and rider loomed out of the darkness. Langford gripped the lines with his left hand and with his right drew a long-barreled revolver.

"Looks like the first battle right now," he said in a low tone to Sage. "If I have to shoot—duck."

A voice challenged, "Langford?"

Langford made no attempt to slacken, pull up his horses. "Who is it?" he called.

Flame lanced toward the buckboard. It was followed instantly by the sharp report of a gun. Harley Langford cried out hoarsely, rose to his feet and pitched from the buckboard to the road.

Sage screamed in anguish and fright, and started to jump from the buckboard to go to her father's aid, but instinct stopped her just in time. The frightened horses were running completely wild.

She was aware that the buckboard tore past a horseman. She gave him a fleeting glance, but he was faceless. He either wore a mask or had his face hunched down into his turned-up coat collar.

She was bounced around by the jolting buckboard and only by clinging to the dashboard was she able to keep from being thrown to the road. But once having hold of the dashboard, she got down on her knees and, groping about, found the lines that her father had dropped. She gathered them up, braced herself, and found the seat.

She had handled horses from childhood and it was only a matter of a minute or so before she had the runaway team under control. By that time, however, they had gone almost a quarter of a mile beyond where her father lay beside the road.

Sage turned the horses and put them into a gallop back up the road. After awhile she pulled them down to a swift walk and began searching the ground beside the road.

She found Harley Langford, a limp huddle. Tying the lines to the dashboard she jumped to the ground. A quick step or two and she was down on her knees.

She touched Harley Langford and a cry was torn from her throat. He was unconscious but alive. Badly wounded, but still living.

How Sage got her father into the buckboard she could not have told later. Harley Langford weighed over two hundred pounds and Sage, despite her lithe strength, weighed little more than half of that. Desperation, however, gave her strength. She maneuvered the buckboard up beside her father, then raised him to a sitting position, with his back against a front wheel. She stooped then and, putting her arms about Langford, pulled upward with the last bit of her strength. She got him up to his limp feet and held him like that for a long moment, using the buckboard for support, for herself as well as Langford. Then she slowly moved to one side, still retaining her grip on her father. Finally she allowed him to lean sidewards, resting the upper part of his body against the buckboard so that it tilted inward and over the floorboard.

That took some of the weight off Sage and she managed, by holding with one hand only, to clamber up on the buckboard beside Langford. Had the horses moved at that moment, Langford would have been thrown to the ground once more, but the animals stood still and Sage found herself in the buckboard with the upper part of Langford's body resting on the floor. She slipped her hands under his armpits then, and pulled him aboard inch by inch until she had his feet clear of the wheels. But his body was too long to ride in that position and she was compelled to seat him on the floor, with his head and shoulders leaning against her.

In that position, with one arm about him, Sage turned the horses and drove them toward the H-L Ranch five or six miles away.

Sage would remember that drive the rest of her life. Her anxiety for her father made her want to put the horses into a dead run, yet she realized the jolting would be too much for him. So she had to control herself. When there was a smooth, straight stretch of road she let out the horses and pulled them in when the road became rough. It took her almost an hour to make the trip and during that time Harley Langford never once regained consciousness, although he let out a groan once or twice.

As she finally approached the house she began calling, but it wasn't until she had stopped before the office building that someone appeared. And then it was Reb Jenkins, who had left the dance in Meadowlands only a few minutes before her.

He cried out when he saw the form of Harley Langford resting on the floorboard of the buckboard. "Who did it, Sage?"

"I don't know," Sage replied. "A masked rider, but there isn't time for that. Get someone to help me take him into the house—and start a rider for Meadowlands for Dr. Kern."

Reb ran off for the bunkhouses, yelling at the top of his voice and men began converging upon the buckboard. Sage supervised the carrying in of her father and then collapsed onto a sofa in the living room from sheer exhaustion.

She was lying there when Emmett Langford came storming in. "What's happened to Dad, Sage?" he cried. "Someone just told me he's been wounded."

Sage regarded him bitterly. "Where've you been all evening?"

"What's that got to do with it?"

"Plenty. If you'd gone along with us like Dad asked you to this wouldn't have happened."

Emmett gave his foster sister an angry look and disappeared into the bedroom where Reb Jenkins was supervising the removal of Harley Langford's clothes.

The foreman of the H-L shook his head when he saw the wound. The bullet had gone into Langford's left side at an angle that led toward the spine. A careful turning over of Langford revealed the fact that the bullet was apparently still lodged inside him. An operation would have to be performed, a delicate one. The blood had coagulated at the opening of the wound and prevented much bloodshed.

Emmett Langford stood at the side of the bed looking down at the man he had called father for most of his life. A fine film of perspiration covered his face. Then without a word he turned and strode back to the living room of the ranch house.

Sage was just getting up from the couch. "He won't live till morning," Emmett said harshly.

Sage exclaimed poignantly, "Oh, no!"

"I'll get the man who shot him," Emmett said savagely. "I'll get him if it's the last thing I do on this earth."

"Yes," Sage said bitterly, "you'll get him and you'll die yourself."

"I'm not afraid to die if I can take him with me."

Emmett strode up to Sage. "Didn't you see him at all? Didn't he speak?"

"Yes, he called out. Asked if it was Dad." Sage frowned. "He only spoke one word, 'Langford,' but the voice was disguised."

Emmett caught hold of her arm. "Disguised! That means he was afraid you'd recognize him. It was someone we know."

"That doesn't help any. We know half the people in the valley."

"But what was his general appearance—was he tall or short, heavy or slender . . . ?"

"It was dark, I tell you. I got the impression somehow that he was fairly tall, at least he seemed to loom up in the saddle. And I wouldn't say that he carried much weight." She stopped suddenly. "He was at least a hundred feet away, though, when he fired."

"He shot only once—from a hundred feet? In the dark?"

"Yes."

"Then he was one hell of a good shot!"

"That thought just occurred to me. Where—where was Sam Sloane this evening?"

"Sloane!" Emmett shook his head. "No, you're wrong there, Sage. It couldn't have been Sloane. He hasn't been around since yesterday. Dad sent him off somewhere."

"Where?"

"I don't know. I saw Sam before he left and he said he'd be gone two-three days, but he wouldn't tell me where he was going, except that Dad was sending him. I—I asked Dad this morning and he told me it was none of my business." Emmett suddenly snapped his fingers.

"This gun fighter, Jim Ralls . . . !"

Sage's eyes narrowed, then suddenly she shook her head. "No—he was in Meadowlands when we left."

"He could have passed you in the dark."

"Nobody passed us on the road."

"He could have cut across country."

"I doubt it. We left Meadowlands at a good clip and Dad kept the horses on a run all the way. It—it happened only two or three miles from town. At the rate we were going, no one could have left town after we did and cut across country and stopped us at the place we were stopped." Sage's eyes suddenly narrowed and as she peered into Emmett's face: "Emmett, where were you tonight?"

Emmett stared at her. "Now, look here, Sage, if you think—"

"Don't be a fool, Emmett. But something you said a minute ago just penetrated. The name of that gun fighter . . . Jim Ralls . . ."

"That's who he is, isn't he?"

"Yes, but—he wasn't exposed until this evening."

"I know it. It happened in Cagle's saloon, when Sheriff Cherry tried to arrest him."

"You were at Cagle's Place tonight?"

"For a little while. I—I got home about an hour ago."

"If you were in town how come you weren't at the dance? I never knew you to miss before."

Emmett scowled. "If you must know, I was calling on a girl in town."

"Who?"

"It doesn't matter; nobody important. All right, it was that redheaded girl who runs the millinery shop—Sue Matson."

"You've been calling on Sue? For how long?"

"This was the first time. I—I saw her in town yesterday and we got to talking, and well, I stopped in to see her tonight." Emmett grunted. "But don't go visualizing wedding bells. We didn't hit it off very well."

"You could do a lot worse. Sue's a very nice girl."

"She's not my style." Emmett grinned at her. "I like 'em with more fire. Like you."

"What?"

"Well, you're *not* my sister, you know."

Sage stared at him in astonishment. "Since when did this start?"

"Oh, I don't think I've been unaware of you at any time, Sage. I always figured there was plenty of time, then Reb began sparking around—"

"Stop it, Emmett!"

"Why?" he asked boldly. He caught her hand. "I'm not going to let you throw yourself away on a man like—"

Sage pulled her hand from Emmett's. "I don't think this is the time for love-making. With Dad lying in the next room . . ."

She turned away from him and went toward the bedroom. Emmett scowled when the door closed on her.

Reb Jenkins came out of the bedroom shaking his head.

"What do you think, Reb?" Emmett asked.

"Looks bad, Emmett," the foreman said. "Ain't no use kiddin' ourselves." He chewed at his lower lip. "I suppose we might as well face the situation."

"That he—might—die?"

Reb nodded. "What do we do?"

"I don't think I get your meaning, Reb?"

"I mean," Reb said slowly, "do we go on?"

"With the ranch? What else is there to do?"

"I meant the fight with the rest of the valley. You heard how the meetin' came out, didn't you?"

Emmett started to nod, then caught himself. "I suppose Dad told them . . . to go to hell."

"He threw it in their faces." Reb nodded toward the bedroom. "And they fired the first shot."

Emmett said darkly: "We'll see who'll fire the last."

The foreman hesitated. "There's something I'd like to know, Emmett. Just in case—well, suppose the old man doesn't come around . . . who gives the orders?"

"You're the foreman."

"Yes, but . . . who gives *me* the orders? You or . . . Sage?"

Emmett exclaimed, "Damn you, Reb, it's just like you to bring it up that I'm not really Harley Langford's son."

"Well, you aren't and you might as well face it."

"You fool," Emmett said hotly. "Don't you know that Dad—yes, *Dad* always regarded me, treated me as if I was his son? There's never been any difference between us. Sage is his daughter and I'm his son."

Reb looked thoughtfully at Emmett. "It's like that in his will? You share equally?"

"I don't know anything about a will. But I'm sure Dad never meant it any other way."

"Maybe he didn't, but if he never got around to making out a will, it's his blood relative that inherits. And that's Sage—not you."

Emmett took a couple of steps to one side and looked sharply at Reb, with turned head. "And if Sage marries you that puts you in the saddle!"

"I wasn't thinking of anything like that."

"The devil you weren't!"

"I was thinking of Sage—inheriting a range war."

Outside, horses' hoofs clopped on the hard-packed earth. Emmett strode to the door. "The doctor . . ."

He whipped open the door. Light from the living room revealed two horsemen just dismounting. Neither was the doctor. One was Sam Sloane. The other was a heavy-jowled, swarthy man of about forty-five.

Sloane came first to the door. He was chuckling wolfishly. "Howdy, Reb. Hi, Emmett. Like you to meet an old friend of mine . . . Roy Dorcas."

"Dorcas!" exclaimed Emmett Langford.

The heavy-jowled man stepped around Sloane. "Dorcas, the outlaw," he said cheerfully. "And you'll be the cub, Emmett." He shook his head. "Don't take after—after Harley."

"You know Dad?" Emmett asked narrowly.

"Know him?" The outlaw grunted. "Knew him ever since I was knee-high to a duck, although I ain't seen him in years. Not since I—well, since Harley became so dad-blamed respectable!"

Ten

———••◆••———

DR. KERN came shortly before eleven o'clock and remained with Harley Langford for more than two hours. His face was sober when he came out of the bedroom.

Pressed by Sage, he reluctantly confirmed the seriousness of Langford's condition. "The bullet's lodged against his spine. He should be operated upon but I'm afraid to chance it without hospital facilities."

"But is there any chance for him if you don't operate?" Sage cried.

"It's hard to say; he's still unconscious. Which is good for him at the moment. In the morning he may be stronger."

"In the morning he may be dead," Emmett interposed.

"If I operated now," Dr. Kern said, "he wouldn't have one chance in—in ten. Wait until morning."

And wait they did, through the long night. Dr. Kern spent most of the time with the patient and at sunrise informed Sage and Emmett that Harley Langford was recovering consciousness. But it was another hour before he finally opened his eyes.

For a moment he stared at the ceiling, then his eyes met Sage's.

"He didn't . . get you!" he said weakly.

Sage shook her head, trying to smile through the tears

68

that filled her eyes. A little smile flitted across Langford's face, then his eyes sought the face of Dr. Kern.

"What does it look like, Doc?"

"Fine," Dr. Kern replied with forced cheerfulness. "Just fine."

"You lie like hell," Langford retorted. He was silent for a moment, then: "I've got to know. There are things to be done. There's . . ." A sudden expression of horror came to his eyes. "Doc, I can't move . . . !"

The doctor turned quickly to Sage and Emmett. "Would you mind leaving us alone for a few minutes?"

Sage and Emmett filed out of the room. Ten minutes later Dr. Kern came out and nodded to Emmett. "He wants to talk to you."

Emmett went into the bedroom. The doctor cleared his throat and went to the window. Sage exclaimed poignantly, "There's no hope, then!"

Dr. Kern turned from the window. "On the contrary, Sage, there's quite a bit of hope."

"Then . . . why . . . ?"

The doctor coughed. "I said there was quite a bit of hope . . . for his life. Unfortunately, well, it's the bullet that's pressing against his spine. It's—paralyzing him."

"That's what he meant when he said he couldn't move."

Dr. Kern nodded. "It's the lower half of his body." He added hastily, "Of course it may be all right in a day or two. I can't tell at this time. All we can do is wait and hope."

Emmett Langford came out of the bedroom and started for the front door. Sage looked at him questioningly. "Does he want to talk to—to me?"

"Not yet." Emmett opened the door. "He asked me to call in Roy Dorcas."

"The outlaw!"

Sage's eyes widened in surprise, but Emmett went outside and a moment later returned with the outlaw chieftain.

Dorcas sized up Sage insolently as he passed through the room to enter the bedroom.

Emmett went in with him and closed the door. They remained inside for ten minutes, with Dr. Kern looking at his watch repeatedly. Finally he shook his head. "I don't think he should talk any more now."

He knocked on the bedroom door, then entered. A moment later he reappeared with Emmett and Roy Dorcas. Dorcas smirked at Sage and left the house. Emmett started to follow but Sage stopped him.

"Just a moment, Emmett, I want to talk to you."

"Can't it wait until later?"

"No, it can't."

Dr. Kern picked up his bag. "I gave him a sedative; he'll go to sleep again. I've got to go into town for some drugs, but I'll be back in two or three hours. He won't waken before then."

He went out and Emmett looked longingly at the door as if he wanted to follow. But then he faced Sage.

"Yes?"

"What . . . did he say?"

"Nothing important. Just gave me some orders about the ranch."

"What orders?"

"The usual stuff."

"Emmett!" exclaimed Sage. "You're lying. He didn't need Roy Dorcas in the room just to give you the usual ranch orders."

Emmett frowned. "I don't think I should tell you, Sage. The less you know the better you'll—"

"What do you think I am—a child?" Sage cut in. "I've a right to know what's going on. As a matter of fact, Dad told me all about it this evening. The range war—"

"He told you? Then you should be able to make a good guess as to what we talked about a few minutes ago."

"He didn't tell me about Dorcas."

Emmett smiled thinly. "Dorcas is our ace in the hole. He's got a dozen men staked out nearby. These two-bit ranchers are going to get the surprise of their lives."

"Dad hired Dorcas to fight for the H-L?"

"Why not?"

A frown furrowed Sage's forehead. "But they're outlaws."

"What do you think some of the people are that Rudabaugh and Macfadden and Allison hired? This Jim Ralls, for example."

"What makes you think he's with them? Ralls, I mean."

"It's a cinch he isn't working for us."

"It doesn't necessarily mean that he's on their side if he isn't on ours."

Emmett's nose wrinkled in disgust. "That kind's always on one side or the other. I wasn't impressed at all by that fight he's supposed to have had with Ben Rudabaugh last night. A fist fight! Ralls' kind doesn't fight with fists."

"Does Sloane?"

Emmett's eyes narrowed. "Why Sloane?"

"He's a killer, isn't he? And what about Roy Dorcas?"

Emmett exclaimed, "What're you driving at, Sage?"

"People who live in glass houses shouldn't throw stones. *We've* hired killers."

"We've hired some men, yes," Emmett said angrily. "To defend our property. We didn't start this fight. We don't want it. We want to keep our property; they want to take it away. We've a right to hire men to protect our property."

"I didn't say we didn't have a right. I was just questioning the *kind* of men we hired. Killers. I don't like it. And I mean to tell Dad what I think about it . . ." She winced. "When he's feeling better."

"That'll be a long time." Emmett chewed at his lower lip. "And you may as well know, Sage, Dad said I was to

ჟe in charge.'' He hesitated. ''And not just until he gets better.''

It took a moment for the significance of the last remark to sink in, but then Sage looked at Emmett sharply. ''What do you mean by that?''

''Just what I said. If he—well, if he dies, I'm to run the ranch.'' He felt it necessary to add: ''All right, I know I'm not his son, but that doesn't seem to make any difference to him.''

''It never has,'' Sage said. She felt the color flow into her cheeks. ''And it never has with me, Emmett. I've always thought of you as my brother.''

Emmett scowled. He took a half step toward Sage, then thought better of it.

Eleven

JIM RALLS strapped his bedroll onto the pack horse, mounted the old gelding and rode out of the clump of cottonwoods that had been his camping ground for the last two nights. He was hungry and put his horse into a swift lope that ate up the three miles to the town of Meadowlands.

He tied his animals to the hitchrail outside Ella's Cafe and entered the restaurant. There were two or three customers in the place, but Ella Snow came at once to wait on him.

"You left kind of early last night," she said.

"So did everybody else."

She nodded. "You've heard the news, of course."

"About the range war?"

"Well, yes, but . . . Harley Langford, I meant."

"What about him?"

"He was shot last night on the way home."

Ralls exclaimed softly, "And the girl—Sage?"

Ella Snow shook her head. "Only her father." She looked soberly at Ralls. "You danced with her."

"Do they know who shot Langford?"

"A masked rider, according to the story that's going around. I understand it's nip and tuck with Langford and even if he lives, he's going to be paralyzed." She hesitated. "She *is* beautiful, isn't she?"

"Who?" Ralls grimaced lightly. "Oh, you mean Sage Langford."

"Who else are you thinking about?"

Ralls regarded Ella steadily. "It's not for me, Ella."

She began polishing the counter with a cloth. "Why not?"

"I've never thought much of the future. Your hand can't be fast all the time. And you can't always see behind you."

"You can quit."

"I can't."

"Why not?"

"Because . . ." Ralls hesitated. "Because I can't."

"There's another hill to the west? You've got to see what's on the other side of it? And when you get on the other side, you'll see still another hill and you'll have to see what's behind *that* one."

"No," Ralls said. "I've never been curious about those valleys on the other side of the hills. I could settle down in any one of them and never ride out of it. Only . . . I made a promise to a man. I can't stop until I fulfill it."

"This man isn't able to do this job himself, which means he's dead."

"He died saving my life."

Sheriff Cherry came into the restaurant and approached Ralls. "Saw your horses outside, Mr. Ralls," he said.

Ralls nodded. Ella Snow went off to the kitchen. The sheriff fidgeted. "Uh, you said last night you'd show up at the judge's court this morning."

"I'll be there."

The sheriff cleared his throat noisily. "The judge is there now."

"I haven't had my breakfast yet."

The sheriff's face was a bright pink. The judge had

apparently sent him out to bring in Ralls, but his fear o.
the man was such that he quaked in his presence.

"Would you mind, after you have your breakfast, uh—
stepping over . . . ?"

"All right," Ralls said pleasantly enough. "I'll make
an appearance."

So a half hour later, Ralls left the restaurant and crossed
the street to the two-story building that housed the jail on
the ground floor and the court on the second floor. A half
dozen townsmen were loafing about outside and the sheriff, who spied Ralls from the platform outside the courtroom, hurried down the stairs.

"We're ready for you, Ralls."

Ralls climbed the stairs and entered the courtroom, a
building about twenty by thirty feet, containing a few
chairs and a table at one end, behind which Judge Gordon
sat. There were a half dozen men in the room, but Ralls
recognized none of them.

The judge looked grimly at Ralls. "I was just going to
send out for you."

"I said I'd be here."

Judge Gordon pointed at the gun that swung in Ralls'
holster. "This is a courtroom. You can't wear a gun in
here."

Ralls made an impatient gesture. "Let's get on with the
business."

"You'll have to surrender that gun before we proceed."

"And let somebody take a pot shot at me when I
leave?"

"It'll be returned to you . . . *if* you leave."

Ralls looked around the ring of hostile faces and hesitated, but then he surrendered the gun to Sheriff Cherry. He
grinned wryly as the sheriff examined the gun butt to count
the notches and found none on it.

The judge banged his table with a small wooden mallet.

"Court will come to order. Case of one Jim Ralls, Sheriff, what is the charge?"

"Why, you know what it is, Judge," Cherry said. "You made me serve the warrant."

The judge scowled. "Jim Ralls, you're accused of murdering Kirby Jenkins. Guilty or not guilty?"

"Not guilty, by reason of self-defense," Ralls said.

Judge Gordon looked around the courtroom. "Harley Langford, who made the charge, isn't able to be here, but where's his foreman, Reb Jenkins?"

"Was he supposed to be here?" the sheriff asked naively.

"Damn it, yes," snapped the judge. Then he saw Fred Anson and pointed his mallet at him. "You, Anson, weren't you a witness to the shooting of Kirby Jenkins?"

Anson looked uncomfortably at Jim Ralls. "I—I guess I was."

"What do you mean, you guess?" the judge demanded. "Were you or weren't you there?"

"Yes."

"Yes, what?"

"Yes, I was there."

"Very well, then tell the court exactly what happened."

Anson screwed up his face. "You mean all of it, about Ellis, too?"

"What's Ellis got to do with this?"

"It was on account of hangin' him that the fight started."

The judge grimaced. "Confine your testimony to the actual crime."

"Which crime?" Ralls interposed. "The attempted hanging of Ellis?"

The judge banged his gavel on the table. "The prisoner will remain quiet." He nodded to Anson. "Proceed."

Les Cagle entered the room and took a position in the rear. He caught Ralls' eye and nodded pleasantly.

Fred Anson cleared his throat. "There ain't much more

to tell. Ralls said we, I mean, they couldn't hang Ellis and then they went for their guns."

"Now wait a minute, Anson," the judge said. "I just told you a moment ago to confine your testimony to the actual crime. Now, think carefully before you answer this question. Who drew first, Kirby Jenkins or the prisoner?"

Fred Anson looked at Jim Ralls, then turned to face the judge, his eyes cloudy. "Everybody drew about the same time, but Ralls beat us."

"I said to think carefully before you answered," the judge said testily. "Did Kirby Jenkins draw first, or did Ralls, the prisoner?"

"No," Anson said.

"No, what?" cried the judge.

"If anybody drew first it was Reb. Kirby had the rope in his hands. He might have started to draw first, but on account of the rope, Reb was ahead of him, I guess."

"For the last time, Anson," Judge Gordon gritted, "did Ralls, or did he not, go first for his gun?"

"I told you," replied Anson. "Reb said it was as easy to hang two as one and then he went—"

"That'll do!" howled Judge Gordon. "It's obvious that the witness is too confused—or too stupid—to testify intelligently. Lacking competent testimony, I see no alternative but to—"

"Just a moment, Judge," called Les Cagle. "It's true that Harley Langford is in no condition to appear in this court and testify, but there's the matter of his shooting."

"What's that got to do with this case?"

"Quite a lot. Ralls knew that Langford had sworn out the warrant against him; they had words about it at the dance hall last night. Then Langford left to ride home. There were at least twenty people who saw him go—and who saw Ralls ride after him."

Ralls stared at Cagle in astonishment. The saloonkeeper

smiled thinly. He said in a low tone: "I told you there couldn't be any neutrals."

Judge Gordon said: "You make out a strong case against Ralls, Mr. Cagle."

Cagle made a gesture that took in everyone in the room. "Practically all of these people can back me up."

The judge nodded. "I can myself." He coughed. "The case against Ralls for murdering Kirby Jenkins can't be concluded at this time because of lack of witnesses. But there's certainly a good case against him and in addition to that, there's this Langford matter. I don't see how I can do anything but remand the prisoner to the custody of the sheriff, to be held in jail until both matters can be investigated more thoroughly."

Ralls took a quick step forward. "You can't lock me up."

The judge banged his table with the wooden mallet. "That's contempt of court."

Ralls moved sidewards, lunging for the sheriff who had his gun, but Les Cagle stepped in between them, the fingers of his right hand touching the lapels of his coat. "Hold it, Ralls!" he said sharply.

Sheriff Cherry pointed Ralls' own gun at him, but his hand was none to steady. "You're under arrest," he said with a slight quiver in his tone.

Ralls paid no attention to the sheriff, but his eyes remained on Cagle's hand. The saloon man had a gun in a shoulder holster. Ralls had made a mistake; he should never have surrendered his gun. Well, he had to pay for that mistake.

"I guess I lose this one," he said.

"Think there'll be another round?" Cagle asked sardonically.

Judge Gordon got up from behind his table and came around. "Take him away," he ordered the sheriff. "And don't take any chances with him. He's a desperate man."

The sheriff knew that well enough, and had no liking for

his task, but with the roomful of men watching him, he braced himself and flourished Ralls' gun.

"All right, prisoner, come along now."

Ralls moved toward him and the sheriff sidestepped quickly. Ralls went out and down the stairs with the sheriff, Cagle and several others following.

Twelve

THE sheriff's office and jail occupied the first floor of the building. The office was a small room containing a roll-top desk and a couple of chairs. A door from this room led to the jail section, which consisted merely of a narrow corridor and two iron-barred cells.

One of these cells was occupied by a middle-aged range tramp. The door of the other stood open and Ralls was herded into it. The sheriff swung the door shut, locked it, and exhaled heavily.

"I guess this'll hold you awhile, Mr. Bad Man!"

Ralls grinned at the man's sudden bravado. He looked at the cot on which was dumped a moth-eaten Confederate Army blanket. As the sheriff went out and closed the door leading to his office, Ralls seated himself on the cot and looked through the bars at the man in the adjoining cell.

The oldster grinned. "Welcome to our little jail, neighbor. My name's Jake Banner. That is, it is up here in Utah. Down in Texas it's somethin' else but I ain't sayin' what."

Ralls regarded the loquacious one sourly, but made no comment. Banner came up to the bars that separated him from Ralls.

"Cheer up, partner. The grub ain't bad at all and it's brought right to you three times a day."

"I'd rather go and get my own," Ralls retorted.

"Yeah, but then you'd have to pay for it." The other prisoner winked. "This is the third time I been in this year. They're making me get out tomorrow, but they can't keep me out." He grunted. "Know what I do outside? Mop floors, sweep, wash dishes, eleven-twelve hours a day. For my grub and a couple of greenbacks, which I spend for whiskey. Silly, ain't it? Here I get my food and I don't need any money because I can't drink anyway. An' I just lay down all day and think."

"What do you think about?"

"Everything. What's wrong with people, things like that." He looked shrewdly at Ralls. "What're you in for?"

"Murder."

The man in the other cell whistled softly. "Murder! That's bad."

"There's nothing worse than murder."

"You can say that again. Uh, they got a case against you?"

"Good enough, so that they'll hang me—if I don't get out of here."

"You figure to escape?" Ralls shook his head and Jake Banner went on, "Because if you are, it can be done."

"How?"

"That's one of the things I been thinkin' about while I been layin' here. Of course, in my case it ain't a matter of escapin', you understand. My problem's how to stay; but just in case a man did want to escape—"

"Get to the point, man."

"It's when the sheriff brings the grub. It's on a tray and there ain't no hole to hand it through the bars. He's a mite skittish and he sets the stuff on the floor out there, then unlocks the door. Then he swings open the door and slides the tray through the door, all the time he's watchin' you and holdin' his gun with the other hand.''

Ralls frowned. ''If he's that careful I don't see how there's much chance to make a break.''

Jake Banner beamed. ''That's because you ain't had time to think about it like I have. Look, he's unlocked your door and he's stooped over, pushin' the tray through the door—*your* door, see—and at that time I let out a yell over here. Ain't no man on earth can help but look off when a sudden yell like that rips out. That's when you make your break.''

Ralls studied the door and finally shook his head. ''He's only looking off for a split second and I'm sure he wouldn't open the door of this cell unless I was in the back end of it. There isn't enough time for me to cross the cell, get through and get his gun before he looks back . . .''

''Look at the door again!'' cried the man in the other cell: ''It opens outwards. You make one jump from the back of the cell. All right, he hears you but he's behind the iron door, see? You make one jump, kick the door one awful kick—and the door does the rest. Get it?''

Ralls stepped quickly toward the door, his eyes gleaming. He looked it over, then retreated to the far end of the cell. Standing there he took a quick forward jump, swung out his right foot. It banged against the steel barred door. He nodded in satisfaction.

''It'll work, old-timer.'' He looked thoughtfully through the bars into the adjoining cell. ''But what about you?''

The oldster chuckled. ''Can I help it if I get a sudden pain in my stomach?''

''They won't believe it.''

''So what're they going to do—keep me in jail thirty days more? That's what I want.''

Thirteen

HARLEY LANGFORD slept through the day, but Sage, although she had not gone to bed all night, found sleep impossible. Throughout the morning she remained in the house, tiptoeing to her father's room and peering in, every now and then. At noon she had a light lunch, then feeling the need of air, she went out and headed for the corrals.

Sam Sloane materialized from the direction of the bunkhouses. "Boss okay?" he asked smoothly.

"He's still sleeping. Would you have my filly saddled?"

Sam Sloane pursed up his lips. "You're not figuring to ride to Meadowlands?"

Sage regarded him coolly. "Why?"

"No reason, only, well . . . I don't think it'd be a good idea."

"Why not?"

"They wouldn't want you to."

"Who wouldn't want me to?"

Sloane scowled. "The kid, I guess."

"Emmett?"

"Yeah."

Sage gave the gunman a long steady look. "I'd like my horse."

83

Sloane whirled on his heel and strode off, but not toward the corral. He entered the nearest bunkhouse.

Annoyed, Sage went to one of the outhouses and found her saddle on a peg. She took it down and was carrying it toward the corral when Reb Jenkins came hurrying toward her. "Where do you think you're going, Sage?" he demanded.

"I'm going for a ride, if it's any of your business."

Reb flushed. "Maybe it ain't any of my business, but I don't think you ought to go riding today."

"Can you give me one good reason why I shouldn't?"

"It might not be healthy."

Angered by this time, Sage threw her saddle over the top pole of the corral and began climbing up herself. Reaching the top, she vaulted lightly into the corral, found a rope hanging over a pole and began coiling it. Her filly watched her from nearby.

Reb came over to the corral. "They said for you to stay here."

"*Who* said?"

"Emmett."

"Emmett isn't *they*."

"All right, Emmett and—and—the new foreman."

Sage stopped and looked sharply at Reb through the corral bars. "What new foreman?"

"Roy Dorcas," Reb said spitefully. "He's running things now."

"By whose authority?"

"Your brother's."

Sage stared at him in astonishment. "Emmett's appointed an *outlaw* foreman of this ranch?"

"That seems to be the idea."

Sage made a sudden, swift throw with the rope and caught the filly by surprise. She led the animal up to the bars and, taking her saddle down from the top pole, threw it over the horse. She began fastening the cinches, letting some of her anger seep out with the physical exertion.

Finished with the saddling, she led the filly to the gate, opened it, mounted and rode through. Reb Jenkins came forward to close the gate.

"I'm going for a ride," she said coldly. "If you wish you can tell my brother *and* the new foreman."

"Tell them yourself," Reb snarled. "And don't try to act so high and mighty with me. I'll still be around after this is all over."

He started for the filly's head, intending to catch hold of the bridle, but Sage swerved the horse away from him and put it into a swift gallop that carried her quickly away from the ranch buildings.

She kept the horse at a gallop until she reached the knoll a half mile from the buildings, when she pulled up and looked back.

She exclaimed aloud as she saw a horse leaving the corrals at a full gallop, heading after her.

Sage turned the filly to the north and gave it its head. But when she looked back over her shoulder she saw the rider from the ranch had cut across diagonally and was within a quarter of a mile of her and coming swiftly.

Angrily, Sage turned again, heading for a clump of cottonwoods this time. The filly tore into them and after a moment, judging that she was out of sight, Sage wheeled sharply and headed back in the direction from which she had entered the trees.

Before she reached the clearing, however, she pulled up and peering through the fringe of trees, saw the pursuer circling the grove. It was Sam Sloane. Sage waited a moment until she estimated that Sloane had completely circled the trees, then sent her horse out into the clearing, heading back swiftly for the knoll she had vacated only recently. When she reached the crest this time she kept going.

Ten minutes later she pulled up her mount and looked

around. She had lost Sam Sloane. She let her horse rest a minute or two, then moved forward again at an easy lope.

She covered two or three miles, passing through herds of Hereford. Sage had grown up within sight of cattle and the absence of them would have been a novelty rather than their presence, so she paid very little attention to the animals. But after passing several herds, something began nagging at her subconscious and she pulled up her horse and watched a small herd of steers.

It was several seconds before she realized what it was about them that had been bothering her. The animals were not grazing. They were nervous and moving in a general direction, eastward. Sage watched them awhile longer and it began to dawn on her that the herd had lately been stampeded. She rode closer to the animals and saw that their hides were wet with perspiration.

Sage looked off toward the west where Horseshoe Valley, a few miles away, opened out into a vast tableland of open desert country. Out in that direction lived the other ranchers: Rudabaugh, Allison, Macfadden, Ellis . . . No, Ellis' buildings had been burned down and Ellis himself seemed to have disappeared.

While she was looking a group of horsemen appeared, skirting a fringe of woodland. Sage watched them for a moment, then turned her horse and rode back in the direction from which she had come. She rode at an easy canter, but suddenly, hearing the drumming of hoofs, looked over her shoulder. The horsemen, some five or six, were pounding after her.

Sage exclaimed softly and, suddenly alarmed, put the filly into a gallop. She had ridden the mount pretty hard and she lacked the speed of a half hour ago. Again looking over her shoulder, she saw that the horsemen had gained.

Off to the left a mile or so was a thick patch of woods. Sage swerved her horse in that direction, hoping that in the cover she could elude her pursuers. She had traveled less than half the distance, when a huge stallion shot across her path.

Seeing that further riding was futile, Sage pulled up her filly. The man on the stallion came toward her and at the same time the horsemen from the rear galloped up.

There were five men altogether, unshaven, dirty. All were strangers to Sage.

She cried out: "What's the idea?"

"A mighty fine-looking filly," said one of the men. But he was looking at Sage instead of her mount.

"Yeah," said another of the men. "Wouldn't think to find something like that ridin' loose on the range."

"It might interest you to know," Sage said coldly, "that this is my father's property."

"Oh, yeah?" sneered one of the men. "First thing you'll be tellin' us that Harley Langford's your old man."

"He is," retorted Sage. "I'm Sage Langford."

The men exchanged quick glances. Then one of them said: "If you're Langford's daughter, what're you doin' way out here?"

"I came for a ride," Sage said, then added firmly: "I go for a ride almost every day."

One of the men said suddenly: "She's lyin'. She wouldn't be out like this with Langford dyin' at home."

"You're right, Bernie," one of the others said. "Anyway, we can't take a chance."

He rode his horse toward Sage, but as he came up, Sage suddenly lashed at his reaching hand with her riding quirt and, driving her heels into the filly's flanks, shot the animal forward, straight at the other men.

Ordinarily, the group would have given way before a charging horse; that is, ordinary men would have given way, but these were not ordinary men. Instead of scattering, they held their horses firmly and Sage's filly crashed into a huge black gelding and a strong arm, grabbing out, caught hold of Sage and tore her from the saddle.

Fourteen

———••————•————•———

THE door leading from the sheriff's office into the jail corridor was pushed open and Sheriff Cherry backed into the room, carrying a tray in each hand with some difficulty.

He let the door swing shut and turned, still balancing the trays. "Dinner," he announced.

Both Jake Banner and Jim Ralls got up from the bunks in their individual cells.

"Don't tell me, Sheriff," Banner said cheerfully. "It's steak and fried potatoes. *And* coffee." He chuckled. "It always is."

The sheriff grunted. He had reached Ralls' cell and, stooping, set the tray on the floor. With the other he moved to Banner's cell, set the tray on the floor, took a big key from his pocket, and unlocked the door. He stepped back quickly, dropping his right hand to the butt of his gun and opening the cell door with his left hand. In that position, watching Banner carefully, he used his foot to slide the tray two feet or so into the cell. The moment the tray was clear of the door he swung the door shut and locked it.

Banner picked up the tray and carried it to his bunk as Cherry moved to Ralls' cell.

The sheriff reached for the lock with his key and saw

that Ralls was standing in the center of his cell. He gestured him back. "Step back."

Ralls moved carelessly back to the bunk, sat down on it, but with his feet firmly on the floor. The sheriff unlocked the cell, drew his gun entirely from the holster and started to pull open the cell door.

At that instant Jake Banner let out a roar of assumed rage.

Sheriff Cherry's head swiveled instinctively and Ralls lunged for the door. Out of the corner of his eye Cherry saw him coming. A cry started to come from his throat. He whirled—and Ralls' body hit the barred door which the sheriff was gripping with his left hand.

The force with which Ralls struck the door was so great that the cell door smashed Sheriff Cherry clear across the corridor and he hit the wall opposite with a thud. He caromed from it to the floor.

A low whistle came from Banner's cell. Ralls, stepping out into the corridor shot a quick glance at Banner. Then he stooped and scooped up the sheriff's gun.

A trickle of blood was oozing down the side of the sheriff's face from a bruise caused by the smashing of the cell door against his face.

Ralls turned to Banner. "How about it, old-timer? You want to come along?"

"Uh-uh," replied Banner. "I like it here."

"Well, so long, then, and—thanks."

Ralls stepped to the door leading to the sheriff's office, opened it and passed through. On the roll-top desk he spied his own Navy gun and picked it up. He examined it, found that it was loaded, and holstered it. The sheriff's gun he deposited on the desk.

He was turning away and starting for the street door when he saw it being pushed open from outside. He stopped and Les Cagle came in.

The saloonkeeper exclaimed, "Be damned!"

"You can try now for that shoulder gun," Ralls said.

Cagle shook his head. His face was a shade lighter than usual and his nostrils flared. "I don't think so," he said.

"Then turn around," Ralls ordered.

Cagle hesitated. "In the back?"

"Isn't that what you expect—after what you did to me?"

A twitch broke Cagle's face. He slowly raised his hands to shoulder level. "I doubt whether Jim Ralls would shoot a man with his hands in the air."

"Turn around," Ralls repeated.

Cagle obeyed and Ralls stepped up to him. Jamming his Navy gun into Cagle's back, he reached over his shoulder with his left hand and flipped out Cagle's holster gun, a short-barreled six-shooter. He looked at the little gun and, grunting, thrust it into the waistband of his trousers.

"I made a mistake this morning, Cagle," he said. "I gave up my gun. Pass the word along, will you, that I'm not giving it up again . . . to anyone."

"You're in the middle, Ralls," Cagle said tonelessly. "Langford's people think you shot him—"

"You suggested that to them."

"All right, they'll still believe it. You've got the H-L against you and you've got us."

Ralls prodded Cagle away from the door. He opened it and was stepping out upon the street, when Cagle added: "And Rance Martindale."

Ralls stopped in his stride, started to turn back into the sheriff's office when a cry broke out across the street.

"Ralls!" a man cried out. "He's escaped from jail!"

Ralls sent a quick glance across the street, saw a man running into a store. He cursed softly and slammed the door of the sheriff's office. Across the street and a hundred feet down in front of Ella Snow's restaurant, stood his saddle and packhorse.

He started across the street running. A half dozen people, seeing him, ducked into doorways.

He was nearing his horses when he saw the restaurant door open; Ella Snow appeared in the doorway. Her face was white and strained.

Ralls reached his horses, snatched at the slip knots that tied them to the rail and was vaulting into the saddle when Les Cagle appeared in the doorway of the sheriff's office, diagonally across the street. A shotgun was in his hands.

Ralls, in the act of mounting at the moment, did not see Cagle. But Ella saw him and cried out: "Look out, Jim!"

Ralls ducked just as Cagle blazed away. The range was pretty far for a shotgun, but even so the charge would have done some damage, for it was aimed high. As it was a couple of the pellets stung Ralls. Then he whipped out his Navy Colt and sent a quick shot across the street that slammed into the door beside Cagle and caused him to leap inside.

Ralls took time to flash a quick smile of thanks to Ella Snow, then turned his gelding out into the street, putting it into a dead run. As he passed the sheriff's office he sent another bullet into the door just to keep Cagle inside.

Behind the gelding pounded the packhorse, running with an easy stride, but keeping its proper position in the rear.

No other shots were fired at Ralls and he cleared the last house of Meadowlands, when he pulled up his gelding and looked over his shoulder. There was no pursuit. It would take time to organize a posse and it would be a reluctant one.

He continued on, following the road as it led from Meadowlands. He rode at a swift trot for a couple of miles, then slackened his horse's speed and began searching the ground at the side of the road. After awhile he saw where a buckboard had been turned in the road and, guessing the cause of it, turned and rode back a few hundred feet, riding bent over toward the side of the road.

Then he found what he was searching for, and stopped and dismounted.

This was the spot where Harley Langford had been shot the night before. Evidence of the ambush was apparent; trampled grass, the scuffing of small shoes and a quantity of half-dried, sticky blood.

Crouched, Ralls studied it all out. Then he turned slowly and began searching the terrain on the far side of the road. There was a small knoll some three hundred yards from the road, rather thickly wooded. The ambusher had taken cover there, no doubt.

Nodding, Ralls straightened and moved to his horse. As he was putting his foot into the stirrup, he suddenly froze. A horse was coming out of the trees on that knoll. On the horse was a man wearing a mask and with a rifle already aimed at Ralls.

Ralls threw himself backwards frantically. The rifle crackled and in front of Ralls his gelding screamed and reared up on his hind legs. Ralls had to spring back to keep from being crushed by the horse as it fell over backwards.

But then he was whipping out his gun and firing at the masked rider. The distance was almost too great for revolver shooting and especially with the would-be assassin already galloping away on his horse, but Ralls sent three shots after him.

He turned to his horse then. The faithful old animal was down, struggling weakly. His wound was mortal, Ralls saw, and a cold rage swept through him. This animal had served him well and faithfully for twelve years—had carried him through the horrors of Gettysburg, the Wilderness, Cold Harbor, Yellow Tavern . . . and thousands of miles in the West. He had gone without food and water many times, had suffered the blazing sun of the desert and broken through crusted snow in mountains.

Two years ago, Ralls had bought the horse he used as a packhorse, an animal now five years old, which could outrun the gelding; a horse with fine breeding behind it. Ralls had used it as a packhorse because of his attachment to the old gelding. The younger horse had learned much from the older animal and was ready at any time to take over its duties. Ralls had simply not had the heart to do it before. But the time had now come.

Swallowing hard, Ralls thrust the gun in his hand at the old gelding's head, and for the first time in his life closed his eyes as he pulled the trigger. When he opened them the gelding was dead. Swiftly then Ralls stripped his saddle from the dead horse. He tore off the pack saddle from the younger animal, dumping all except the blanket roll beside the road. Then he put on the saddle, fastened the blanket roll behind it and mounted. The entire process had taken less than five minutes, but by that time the killer of the gelding was out of sight.

The former packhorse started off at a speed that surprised even Ralls, who knew the animal's capacity. Straight down the road at first, then across country toward a grove of cottonwoods into which Ralls had seen the other horsemen ride. Ralls circled the grove without slackening speed, topped a knoll and far away, more than a mile, saw a tiny horse.

"All right," he said aloud. "Now we'll see!"

He touched the swiftly moving animal under him and the horse responded with a fresh burst of speed. A few minutes later the horse ahead became a horse and rider and Ralls estimated that the distance between them was about three-quarters of a mile.

He rode loosely in the saddle, bent slightly forward. His horse was running easily, even though he had already run almost two miles. He was good for much more distance, and perhaps even a brief charge at the finish.

For two or three minutes the distance between Ralls and the other rider did not decrease and Ralls guessed that he had been seen. The fugitive was whipping up his horse.

Ralls, looking ahead, saw that the country had flattened out. For several miles it was as flat as a race track and without the clumps of cottonwoods that here and there dotted Horseshoe Valley. The man ahead had to ride for it. It was horse against horse.

The man ahead became gradually larger and Ralls knew that his was the better mount. Perhaps the fresher horse, too, for the animal was long rested, having stood all morning upon the street of Meadowlands, whereas the horse ahead had probably traveled several miles before its rider had risked the shot at Ralls.

The distance became less, a half mile, a third, and then a quarter. For a few moments, then, the distance did not decrease and Ralls thought that the man ahead was whipping his animal to its last desperate effort.

They were riding straight down into Horseshoe Valley now, within a quarter of a mile of the northern rim of the mountain. The fugitive could have struck for the mountainside, but evidently feared it too much. At last, however, he was less afraid of it than of his pursuer and swerved his horse sharply and headed straight for the mountain.

Ralls turned his own horse and spoke to it. "This is it," he said, and slapped the animal's right flank with the flat of his hand.

The change in course had given Ralls an advantage. The rider ahead had been a quarter mile in advance of him before making a sharp left turn. But Ralls, in the rear, by turning, could head diagonally toward him and the mountain. Instead of a quarter mile to the spot where the other rider had turned off, then another quarter mile to the mountain range, Ralls had to cover only the long side of the triangle, perhaps three-eighths of a mile. And now he was putting his horse into a burning drive that ate up the distance between him and the man ahead.

Ralls closed up rapidly and, watching the rider and his mount ahead, saw that the horse was weaving and faltering. It was a question whether it could survive the last dash to the mountainside, where the rider evidently intended to make a stand with his back against the slope.

It didn't make it. An eighth of a mile from the sudden rise of the ground the horse collapsed completely. Its rider sprang clear. Ralls, then less than three hundred yards away, swerved his horse to the right as he saw the rider rush back to the horse and claw at the saddle. A rifle came clear in his hands, a shot rang out and the worn horse kicked its last. The killer dropped down behind to use the animal as a shield.

Ralls drew his Navy gun, bent low in the saddle and began a circuit of the dead horse and rifleman. A bullet whined feet over his head. Then another.

Ralls turned his horse to the left, well past his quarry, sent it straight for the mountainside and, within fifty yards of it, turned it left again.

Ralls' opponent was outflanked; but it was still rifle against revolver, at more than two hundred yards. Ralls headed straight for his man, however, firing as he rode.

The man on the ground jumped to his feet, started to climb over his dead horse to get on the far side, then suddenly lost his nerve and threw down his rifle. "Don't shoot!" he yelled. "I surrender!"

The cravenness of the man surprised even Ralls. He rode down at a full gallop, pulled up his horse and vaulted to the ground. And then he finally recognized the man who had tried to kill him.

It was young Emmett Langford.

Fifteen

•••◆•••

"RALLS," the youth said thickly, "d-don't shoot. I—I give up."

"You killed my horse," Ralls said blazing. "And you tried to kill me."

"I—I know," faltered Emmett. "But I—I thought you were someone else. The—the man who shot my father last night."

Ralls stepped up to the young gunman, reached out and plucked the revolver from his holster. Contemptuously he threw the weapon away, then holstered his own gun.

"You're lying," he said.

"I'm not," cried Emmett. "I went to the place where Dad was shot to—to try to pick up a trail."

"And you had to wear a mask to do that?"

Emmett gulped. "It was only a handkerchief."

"What was the point in hiding your face?" Ralls waited for Emmett to answer and when he didn't, he went on: "You know what I think? You shot your father yourself . . ."

"Oh, no!" Emmett cried, a look of terror shooting over his face.

Ralls stepped forward and caught hold of the youth's arm. "Why?"

"I didn't." Emmett howled. "I didn't shoot him."

96

Ralls shook Emmett with one hand and with the other slapped his face hard. "Tell me the truth," he said savagely. "Why did you shoot him?"

Sudden sobs shook Emmett's lean body. Tears welled down his cheeks and he cried like a four-year-old child. Ralls shoved him away in disgust.

And now for the first time in his life Ralls was caught by surprise. He had been so intent in shaking the truth out of Emmett and had believed himself alone with the younger man, in open country, that he had paid no heed to his surroundings, so that he did not see the three men who came down the hillside less than three hundred yards behind him and rode up to within fifty yards.

He wasn't aware of their presence until a voice called out: "Don't reach!"

Ralls stiffened. His instinct was to whip out his gun, whirl and fire, knowing that he would take a bullet to throw one, but he weighed the chances and knew that they were overwhelmingly against him.

Emmett Langford, tears still streaming down his face, leaped back. "Dorcas!" he croaked. "Roy Dorcas."

"Get his gun," a voice behind Ralls said.

Emmett Langford started to reach for Ralls' gun, but met his eye and backed away. "It's—it's Jim Ralls . . ."

"Ralls!" grated the harsh voice of Roy Dorcas. "Well, well . . . !"

He rode up to the right of Ralls and turned his horse. His two men remained behind, one on each side, flanking Ralls.

"Ralls," repeated Dorcas, "caught by the short hair." He made a signal to one of his riders beyond Ralls. The latter heard the man dismount and approach him. He tensed for a moment and wondered if he could control himself.

The emergency passed quickly. A hand snatched the revolver from his holster and Ralls was at the mercy of the outlaws. Dorcas rode up closer then, chuckling wolfishly.

"I missed you at Cheyenne when they were building the railroad," he said. "And they were still talking about you at Green River when I was there three or four years ago."

"I'd just as soon have missed you this time," Ralls retorted coldly.

"Oh, I don't doubt it," Dorcas said. "I'm no man-to-man fighter like those fools who've gone up against you. I've lasted a long time because I've got a crowd of men and I let them do the work." He shook his head. "Too bad, I could have used a man like you."

"I'll take care of him, Dorcas!" Emmett Langford suddenly cried. He began searching the ground for his gun which Ralls had thrown away a few minutes ago.

Dorcas chuckled. "You weren't doing so good awhile ago."

Emmett saw his gun some thirty or forty feet away. He scurried over, pounced on it, turned and came menacingly toward Jim Ralls.

"Now, Mister Bad Man," he cried, "let's see you do some begging."

Ralls looked at Emmett from under lowered brows. This could well be the most perilous position of his entire life. His gun had been taken away from him, he was in the power of a ruthless outlaw and a crazy youth was advancing on him with a gun in his hand. Yet Ralls was helpless to do anything about his predicament. He remained motionless and Emmett came up to within a dozen feet of him.

"Get down on your knees," Emmett gritted. "Get down and beg for your life." He flourished the gun and suddenly sent a bullet singing inches past Ralls' head.

"I mean it," he said thickly. "I'm going to kill you, anyway, but before I do you're going to get down on your knees."

The scene was pretty strong even for the three outlaws.

They exchanged glances and Dorcas, frowning, said: "Now, wait a minute, Emmett. I don't think—"

"You heard what Dad said," Emmett cut in. "I'm only doing the job he wanted you to take care of."

"What about Rance Martindale?" Ralls asked suddenly.

The name seemed to make little impression on young Langford, but the outlaw chieftain's eyes narrowed. "What was that name you said?"

"Martindale," Ralls said deliberately. "Rance Martindale."

Dorcas stared at Ralls, then shook his head. "Don't know anyone named Martindale."

"Neither do I," snapped Emmett. "And I've had enough of this." He raised his gun.

Roy Dorcas stepped forward and brushed down Emmett's gun hand. "Hold it, Emmett." He caught the young man's arm and led him outside, out of earshot of Ralls. He talked earnestly to Langford for a moment. Emmett replied angrily, but at the conclusion of the talk he strode to one of the outlaws' horses and mounted.

"Hey," cried the outlaw, who owned the horse.

"You'll ride double with O'Sullivan," Roy Dorcas said. He came back to Ralls. "Get on your horse."

Under the watchful eyes of the outlaws, Ralls caught his horse and mounted. Dorcas climbed aboard his own animal and the other two outlaws got on the remaining animal. By that time Emmett Langford was a half mile away, riding across the wide expanse of Horseshoe Valley.

Dorcas took the lead of the small cavalcade, heading straight for the mountainside nearby. He seemed to know where he was going for he soon picked out a narrow shelf that led at an angle up the slope.

After a few minutes the going became rougher and Dorcas dismounted and drove his horse ahead. He followed on foot. Ralls got off his horse and followed. The other outlaws brought up the rear.

The group climbed tortuously for a quarter of a mile, when they suddenly came upon a blind canyon. The ground fell sharply for several yards and rose again on the other side. Dorcas turned into the canyon which seemingly ended a hundred yards away.

Yet when Dorcas' horse reached the blind end it moved straight into a clump of heavy brush and disappeared. Dorcas turned and chuckled. "Not bad, eh?"

He stepped aside and let Ralls' horse pass him, then nodded to Ralls. "Keep close up."

He followed Ralls' horse closely, directly into the brush. Ralls entered and Dorcas moved ahead through the clump of brush and into a narrow ravine less than ten feet wide. This ran for a hundred feet or so and was already being traversed by the horses that had gone ahead.

It, too, seemed to end just ahead, but as they approached Ralls noted that there was actually an opening to the right which had evidently been formed at some remote time by an earthquake and was no more than a wall of rock, cleft in two.

The horses passed through this, brushing both sides as they went, so narrow was it. Dorcas followed, then Ralls. Twenty feet ahead, the horses disappeared and Dorcas waited for Ralls to come up.

When Ralls reached Dorcas he drew in his breath sharply.

Sixteen

STRAIGHT ahead, falling down sharply below them was a small, hidden valley. It was perhaps a quarter mile long and about half that in width and was floored with a lush growth of grass and at the far end a heavy stand of timber.

In the center stood a couple of log cabins. A dozen horses grazed nearby.

"Nice little hideout," Dorcas commented sardonically.

Ralls nodded thoughtfully. "So it is. I'm surprised that a stranger would find it."

Dorcas grunted. "A stranger wouldn't find it in a year, even if he knew it was here and was searching for it."

"But *you* found it?"

Dorcas shrugged and began descending the slope in front of them. A few minutes later they reached the floor of the valley and were seen by the men at the cabins. A couple of them came forward to meet them.

"Roy," one of the two said, as he came up, "the boys brought in a prisoner . . ."

"So did I," Dorcas replied.

The man scowled at Jim Ralls. "The one we already got is prettier. A girl. She . . ." he hesitated. "She claims to be Langford's daughter."

Dorcas exclaimed, "Sage Langford?"

"That's what she says her name is."

"Where is she?"

The outlaw nodded toward the nearer of the two log cabins and Dorcas, muttering, strode quickly toward the cabin. He jerked open the door and went inside.

Ralls, having approached the cabin, stopped. A number of men gathered and examined him curiously with no visible animosity. One of the two men who had captured him winked at his companion.

"Look him over, boys. It's Jim Ralls himself!"

The announcement of the name made about the same impression on the outlaws as if they had suddenly been told that a dozen United States Marshals had surrounded them. Two or three of the men even ducked out of sight behind the log cabins. The others gave Ralls a wide berth until they became aware that he was unarmed. At that, they expressed a disbelief in the prisoner's identity. Then Dorcas reappeared from the log cabin, his face dark in anger.

"Roy," one of the men cried, "Lin here claims this fella's Jim Ralls."

"He's Ralls, all right," snapped Dorcas, "but I'd rather have two Jim Rallses, than that girl inside. Who was fool enough to bring her here?"

One of the outlaws said sullenly: "Wasn't anything else we could do. She saw us—" He shot a quick look in Ralls' direction. "Well, we didn't think it was a good idea to have her tell anyone what we were doin'."

"You could have held her outside the valley, couldn't you? Until you talked to me."

"We were doin' that, Roy," said the other man, "but we saw a bunch of riders comin' our direction and the ground was too open to go anywhere else."

"So you came here! And let them see where you were goin'."

"They didn't see. We waited in the first canyon and watched. They went by without even climbin'."

"How many men?"

"Seven or eight."

Dorcas exhaled heavily. "The harm's done, but I'd give a lot if we didn't have her here."

One of the men, a wicked-looking ruffian, licked his lips with his tongue. "How much, Roy?"

Dorcas looked at the man narrowly. "Don't try anything like that, Bickle. I don't want the girl here, but anyone lays a finger on her answers to me." He gestured about the group. "That goes for all of you."

There was a little grumbling among the men, but they soon dispersed; Dorcas' leadership of the outlaws was unquestioned.

Dorcas signaled to Ralls, then, and led the way to a log that lay on the ground a short distance from the nearest log cabin. He seated himself and looked up at Ralls, who remained standing.

"I think we ought to have a little talk, Ralls."

"I'm not much of a talker," Ralls replied.

"Well, I am," Dorcas said testily. "And if you know what's good for you, you'll talk. I stopped that fool kid from killing you, but you know danged well you're in a tight spot." He glowered at Ralls. "What about Martindale?"

"I thought you said you'd never heard the name."

"I've heard it, all right."

"When?"

Dorcas swore. "Damn it, Ralls, don't try that stuff on me. We're going to talk about Rance Martindale."

"All right," Ralls said suddenly. "Let's talk about him."

"Go ahead. What do you know about him?"

"I know that he disappeared a good many years ago."

"When?"

"Don't *you* know?" Ralls asked.

"You're doing the telling."

"He left Michigan seventeen years ago. He traveled from Council Bluffs to Fort Bridger with an emigrant wagon train, but he left the train at Fort Bridger—to take the Hastings Cut-off, against the advice of everyone in the train. He never reached California."

"A lot of the emigrants didn't," Dorcas said. "The Indians got some of them; some just died on the way and some—well, some of them the Mormons took care of."

"At Mountain Meadows?"

"About a hundred and fifty were killed there."

"That was an Arkansas wagon train. Martindale wasn't with them."

"How do you know he wasn't? He could have run into the train and joined it."

"He didn't."

"How do you know he didn't?"

"Because I've spent nine years looking for Rance Martindale. I haven't done anything else in those nine years."

Dorcas looked at Ralls sharply. "That's a pretty strong statement, Ralls. Seems to me I've been hearing of you doing quite a few things—"

"Side issues, Dorcas. That came out of this."

"Nine years," mused Dorcas. "That would be '65. But you said Martindale disappeared seventeen years ago—'57. Why did it take you eight years to *start* looking for him?"

"Because I never heard of Martindale until 1864."

Dorcas exclaimed and got to his feet. "You're looking for a man you never saw and never heard of?"

"I heard of him in 1864."

"From who?"

Ralls hesitated. "Tom Sutherland!"

Dorcas stared at Ralls. "Who the devil is Tom Sutherland?"

"His sister was married to Rance Martindale."

"Sutherland's sister was married to Martindale, but where do *you* come in?"

"Sutherland was my first lieutenant. He was killed at Yellow Tavern, but before he died I promised him I'd find Rance Martindale . . . and ask him what became of Helen Sutherland, his wife."

Dorcas shook his head in bewilderment. "You've spent nine years looking for a man . . . to keep a promise?"

"Tom Sutherland died saving my life."

"A promise to a dead man," snorted Dorcas. Then his tone changed. "And what if you find Rance Martindale?"

"That'll depend on the answers he gives me—about his wife."

"Suppose she's dead?"

"I'll want to know how she died." Ralls paused. "You see, she had fifty thousand dollars in gold when she left Michigan. It was her money—not Martindale's."

"What's the difference? A woman marries a man, her property becomes his." Dorcas screwed up his face in heavy thought.

The outlaw chieftain began pacing back and forth, his hands clenched behind his back. Ralls seated himself on the log recently vacated by Dorcas.

Finally Dorcas stopped his pacing and looked down at Ralls. "I'm going out for awhile. I may not be back until morning, but you'll be all right until then, unless you try anything fancy. I'm leaving word with the boys." He signaled one of the outlaws who was near the closest log cabin. "Lin, get three-four of the boys and saddle up." He strode toward the log cabin, started to enter, then changed his mind.

Behind him the door opened and Sage Langford appeared. Her eyes went past Dorcas and took in Jim Ralls.

"So," she said, "you're one of them, after all."

Dorcas whirled. "Ralls?" He snorted. "D'you see a gun in his holster?"

The outlaw, Lin, rode up on his horse and leading Dorcas'.

The outlaw leader said, to Sage: "If you're smart you'll stay inside. And it might be a good idea to keep the door locked on the inside."

"You're a fool, Dorcas," Ralls said. "You've lasted a long time, but there are some things you can't do, and keeping a woman prisoner is one of them."

"You'd be surprised what I can do," Dorcas retorted.

Ralls shook his head. "You think the law's been after you, Dorcas; you're used to being a fugitive. Harm her and you'll be hounded like no man on earth's ever been hounded." He made an impatient gesture. "You're riding high now that you've thrown in with Langford, but even if Langford wins over the ranchers you're not safe. Even if Langford dies."

Three riders came up. Dorcas mounted his horse, looked down at Sage. "Do like I tell you." Then, to Ralls: "And you, Ralls, don't try anything."

He turned in his saddle, saw the ruffian, Bickle. "Bickle, I want Ralls here when I come back. I want him alive, but if he makes a move, stop him."

Bickle, a hulking giant, came up to Ralls and struck him a savage blow in the face. Ralls reeled back, dropped to his knees. "You mean like this, Roy?"

Dorcas looked sourly at Bickle. "Just keep him here."

He prodded his horse and the animal moved forward. The four men who were going with him followed at a trot. Ralls got to his feet and looked at Bickle, whose hand was on the butt of the gun. Bickle pointed at the second log cabin.

"Git in there!"

Ralls wiped a trickle of blood from his mouth and started for the cabin. He gave Sage a meaningful look and she stepped back into her own cabin, closing the door.

The cabin Ralls entered was about a dozen feet wide and perhaps twenty long. It was made of logs set up on end and chinked with mud and grass. Most of the chinking had fallen out and the logs were pretty pulpy from age.

Three or four sagging bunks were along the walls and a rough table stood in the center of the room. There were also three or four short benches made of split logs. These were pulled up to the table by four outlaws who were engaged in a noisy game of cards.

Bickle pointed to one of the bunks. "Sit down," he said. "The less we hear from you the better I like it."

Ralls seated himself on one of the bunks, and after a moment leaned back and closed his eyes. But he did not sleep.

Seventeen

IT WAS late afternoon when Emmett Langford reached home. He was met at the door of the ranchhouse by Reb Jenkins and Sam Sloane.

"Sage has disappeared," Reb said, before Emmett had even dismounted.

Emmett's eyes went to Sam Sloane. "I thought I told you to see that she didn't go riding today?"

"That's right, Emmett," Sloane said. "I tried to stop her, but Reb here let her saddle up. I chased her, but she pulled a trick on me and got away." He scowled. "I spent all day ridin' around tryin' to find her."

"Did you try Meadowlands?"

"I sent Al Mokey to town. He says nobody saw her there."

A little frown creased Emmett's forehead, but he erased it quickly. "She knows this range as well as anyone. No chance of her getting lost."

"I wasn't thinking about her getting lost," Reb Jenkins said. "Only Mokey said, when he got back, that the place was like a ghost town. Deserted."

"So?"

"The ranchers are keeping their men at home."

"To make a movement against us?"

"It's their fight, isn't it?"

"They'll get their bellies full of fighting before this is finished. Put some guards out tonight just in case they try anything foolish."

"I've already sent out men," Reb Jenkins said.

"Where to?"

"To keep an eye on the different ranches."

Emmett swore. "What the devil'd you do that for? We need every man right here on this place."

"Langford told me to do it," Reb said sullenly.

"You talked to Dad? When'd he wake up?"

"Two-three hours ago."

Emmett strode into the house and went into Harley Langford's bedroom. The rancher was lying in his bed, fully awake, but with a complete lack of expression on his face.

"Hello, Emmett," he said quietly.

It was characteristic of Emmett that he did not inquire as to the condition of the man he had always called Father. He nodded curtly. "What's this about you telling Reb to send men away from here?"

"Pickets," the older man said. "You've got to have them out."

"But we can't spare the men," Emmett protested. "If those ranchers get together all the men they've got and ride down here in a bunch, we won't have a man too many." His face twisted angrily. "You said this morning that I was to be in charge of the ranch."

Langford said, without heat: "You're an ungrateful pup, aren't you?"

"My interests are yours," Emmett retorted. "You're layin' in bed, you won't have to do any of the fighting."

"Where's Roy?"

"Out in the hills. I ran into him about an hour ago. I put him in the way of capturing Jim Ralls."

"Roy's got Ralls?" Harley Langford asked in sudden excitement. "What's he intend to do with him?"

"Damned if I know. I was going to finish him right then and there but Dorcas wouldn't let me." He scowled. "I think it's about time you told me just what Dorcas has got on you, the way you let him take over."

Langford hesitated a moment. "Dorcas is my brother."

Emmett exclaimed in astonishment, "But he's an outlaw!"

Langford made a small gesture with his hands. "What's an outlaw? Half the people in the West are outlaws. Down in Texas the cattle were running wild. Whoever put a brand on them owned them. The land didn't belong to anyone except the fellow who took it. Some of the biggest ranches in the country didn't cost their owners a dollar. They took the land and put brands on whatever cattle they found. Ten years ago that was the customary thing—today, you do it, you're an outlaw."

"Dorcas has done a lot more than just take cattle."

"There are peace officers who've done as much. They got jobs and that made them respectable. Roy's ready to settle down—"

Emmett's eyes narrowed. "Here?"

"There's enough for Roy, too."

"There isn't enough for both of us."

Langford looked steadily at Emmett. "Frankly, Emmett, you're pretty young to run the H-L. I don't think you—"

Emmett cut in: "I've played second fiddle long enough. I don't want Dorcas here."

"Without him you may not have anything to run at all. The ranchers will take it away from you."

"I don't think they will. I've been doing some thinking. We're spread out too much. My idea's to pull all the men in and keep them around the ranch. Rudabaugh's crowd will think we're afraid of them and they'll come down here. We'll ambush them—"

"Suppose they don't ride into an ambush?"

"They've got to come to us sooner or later."

Langford shook his head. "Nobody ever won a war by retreating and waiting for the other side to come to them. You've got to go out and fight them. Cut out a chunk here, another there. Beat them in sections if you're not strong enough to fight them all at once. Of course you've got to have good men for work like that. And that's where Roy comes in. His men are tough."

"Thieves and cutthroats!"

Harley Langford looked deliberately at the man he had always called his son. "As to that, Emmett, what are you?"

For a moment, Emmett's mouth remained open. Then his face twisted in sudden rage and he whirled and walked out of the room.

In the living room, a fat Mexican woman came out of the kitchen. "You wan' your supper now?" she asked.

"No," said Emmett thickly. He crossed the room and left the house. Outside, he walked to the corrals, where Sam Sloane was unsaddling his horse.

"Leave it saddled," Emmett snapped. "I'm going into town."

"Alone?"

"You can come along if you're not afraid."

Sam Sloane smiled wolfishly. "Now what would I be afraid of?"

"All right, then come on."

Sam Sloane got his own horse and the two men were soon off for Meadowlands, reaching the town shortly after dark.

There were only a few horses hitched to the rails, most of them near Cagle's Saloon. Sloane looked inquiringly at Emmett, but the latter shook his head and headed for a place run by a man named Longnecker, a much smaller saloon than Cagle's.

They entered and discovered only two or three patrons in the place. Longnecker, a sour-faced man of about thirty-five, was behind the bar. He came up, scowling.

"I don't want any fighting in here," he said.

"Nobody's going to fight," snapped Emmett. "I want a drink."

Longnecker hesitated, but finally brought a bottle and glasses. Emmett and Sloane poured out drinks, tossed them off, then poured out fresh drinks. One of the other patrons paid for his drink and started for the door.

"Here, you," Sam Sloane said. "Where do you think you're going?"

"Home," replied the man nervously.

"What's your hurry?"

"I—I promised my wife I'd be home early."

"Oh, let him go, Sam," Emmett said.

"All right," growled Sloane to the man, "but see that you go home, if you know what I mean."

The man left hastily. Sloane shook his head and said to Emmett, "Maybe this wasn't such a good idea, Emmett. If he spreads the word that we're here, we may have a little trouble . . ."

"We can handle it," Emmett said confidently.

They had several more drinks, then the door of the saloon opened and the customer who had left a little while ago came in hesitantly, his face twitching.

"Les Cagle'd like to see you," he said.

Sam Sloane hurled his whiskey glass to the floor. "So you went right to him after I warned you . . ." He reached for his gun and then Longnecker shoved the twin barrels of a shotgun over the top of the bar. "Hold it, Sloane," he snarled. "I don't want any shooting in my place, but if there's got to be some, I'll be the one does it."

"Cagle said to tell you it was all right, he just wanted to

talk to you," Cagle's emissary said quickly to Emmett. "He's got a proposition he wants to put to you."

"I'm not walking into any trap," Emmett said. He looked uneasily at the shotgun that was threatening him and Sam Sloane. "Tell Cagle we'll meet him in Ella Snow's restaurant."

The man bobbed his head and ducked out of the saloon. Emmett whirled on the saloonkeeper. "So you're sidin' with them against us?" he sneered. "It's a good thing to know."

"Yeah," chimed in Sloane, "we won't forget it!"

"Neither will I," Longnecker said defiantly. "Keep out of my place hereafter."

Emmett and Sloane left the saloon and proceeded a few doors up the street to Ella Snow's restaurant, which was entirely deserted save for Ella behind the counter and the Chinese cook out in the kitchen. Ella greeted Emmett without enthusiasm.

"What'll it be?"

"Whiskey," said Sloane, winking at Emmett.

"I don't serve liquor here."

"Well, then how about a kiss?"

"Kisses aren't on the menu today."

Sloane chortled. "Smart girl, ain't she, Emmett?"

Emmett surveyed Ella. He had seen her around for some time, but had never really taken a good look at her. But now his eyes showed interest.

"Yeah," he agreed, "she's smart. And pretty, too." He smiled at Ella. "You run this place alone, don't you?"

Before Ella could reply, the door opened and Les Cagle came in. He smiled at Ella Snow, then took a seat at the counter near Emmett.

"Hello, Emmett."

"What's on your mind, Cagle?"

"Why, I thought it might be worthwhile you and me having a little talk. Private talk."

"Sam's all right."

"I think it'd be better if he'd wait outside."

Emmett hesitated, then shrugged. "All right, Sam, but stay outside, if you know what I mean."

Sloane did not want to leave, but after giving Cagle a significant look he went out. Ella Snow walked back to the kitchen which left Cagle and Emmett alone at the counter.

"All right, Cagle," Emmett growled, then, "Talk."

"How's your father?"

"Good enough."

Cagle cleared his throat. "I guess I should have said your *foster* father."

"You didn't come here to talk about our relationship," Emmett said testily.

"As a matter of fact, I did. There's talk that he hasn't got much chance of pulling through. That leaves you in a rather bad spot, doesn't it? Since you're only his adopted son and Sage is his daughter."

"That's how much you know about it," sneered Emmett. "The H-L will be mine."

Cagle looked sharply at Emmett. "Langford told you that?"

"Who would he leave it to? A woman can't run a ranch like the H-L."

"A woman's husband can. Sage must be twenty-one or so. Old enough to get married. And there are plenty—"

"Sage is marrying *me*," snapped Emmett.

"What about Reb Jenkins?"

Emmett dismissed Reb Jenkins with a wave of the hand. "Sage'll do what the old man wants her to do."

"And he wants her to marry you?"

"Yes."

Cagle hesitated. "That'll still make her the real owner."

Emmett suddenly banged his fist on the counter. "What're you driving at, Cagle?"

"Why, I was thinking about Roy Dorcas, Emmett. There is a rumor that he's showed up."

"What if he has?"

Cagle smiled disarmingly. "I'm going to tell you something that no man in Meadowlands knows." He dropped his voice to a whisper. "I rode with Dorcas years ago."

Emmett stared at Cagle. "How long ago?"

Cagle closed one eye in a deliberate wink. "When Dorcas' brother was with us."

"You know . . . ?"

"Yes!" Cagle hitched up closer to Emmett. "Do you see what I mean now? The girl's got an uncle, a pretty salty *hombre*. Of course if you think you can handle Roy Dorcas *and* the girl—"

"What's your proposition?" Emmett asked tonelessly.

"The H-L Ranch for you, and the rest of it for me."

"What rest?"

"Mcfadden's got a ranch; so has Allison and Rudabaugh and a few others. All together they amount to quite a bit, almost as much as the H-L." Cagle smirked. "I'll be satisfied with them."

"But how're you going to take them?"

"That's the proposition." Cagle grinned. "Who do you think is the leader of the ranchers? Rudabaugh?" He grunted. "All he can think of is smashing somebody with his fists. *I* boss them, Emmett. A little needling, a little flattery and a few dollars here and there and they do what I want them to do. There wouldn't be any range war today if I hadn't put them up to it."

"And now you want to sell them out?"

"Well, isn't that what you're going to do? Sell out Harley Langford?"

Emmett licked his lips and nodded.

Eighteen

————◆—◆—◆————

BICKLE, the outlaw, was no general, but his life had been in danger for so many years that self-protection was instinctive with him. Toward evening he began issuing orders.

"Hogan, take your rifle and get outside the pass."

"What for?" cried Hogan.

"Because I said so." Bickle glowered. "I'm not going to be grabbed while I'm sleeping."

"And I'm not going to sit out there all night," Hogan protested.

"You'll be relieved at midnight." Bickle nodded to another man. "You, Taney, you'll take up a post inside the pass, and Kelso, you'll be outside the cabins here, just in case. At midnight you'll wake up Lloyd, Woodson and Pence and they'll take your places."

"That takes care of all of us," Hogan said sarcastically, "except you, and you sleep all night, I suppose."

"Dorcas left me in charge," retorted Bickle. "You never saw Dorcas standin' guard, did you?"

There was some more discussion, but the guards finally went off to their posts. They took food along with them. After they had gone, the remaining four outlaws cooked their own suppers. They were almost finished eating, when

Bickle suddenly thought of the prisoners. "Here we been cookin'," he said, "when we got a woman here."

He got up from the ground and walked to the cabin in which Sage had locked herself. He banged on the door with his fist. "Hey, you want somethin' to eat?"

There was no reply and Bickle pounded the door again. "C'mon out of there, if you want somethin' to eat!"

Sage's voice came through the door. "I'm not hungry."

Bickle started to turn away, then wheeled and kicked the door. "Open up!"

There was quiet inside the cabin for a moment, then the door opened and Sage stepped into the doorway. She had a thick club of wood in her hand.

The outlaws at the fire guffawed. "Look out, Bickle!" one of them called jeeringly.

Jim Ralls, who had been sitting on the door stoop of the other cabin, got to his feet and moved to the fire around which the three men sat. He stooped and picked up a frying pan that contained some rather limp bacon.

Bickle, spurred on by the jeering of his companions in crime, moved toward Sage. "I said to come and eat, and I mean it," he said angrily.

"And I told you I wasn't hungry," Sage retorted, standing her ground.

"Look out she doesn't brain you," one of the outlaws called.

Goaded, Bickle lunged for Sage. The club came down. Bickle tried to duck under it, but the stick of wood cracked his skull. He staggered back a couple of feet, then recovered, and leaped for Sage. At that moment Ralls threw the frying pan. It struck the outlaw on the side of the head, splattering some of the bacon grease on Sage nearby.

The frying pan was an iron one and caught Bickle squarely. He fell sidewards to his knees. For a moment he remained in a kneeling position, while he cleared the fog from his brain. Then, with a roar, he came to his feet, clawing for his gun.

Ralls started for Bickle, but one of the other men leaped in between, with drawn gun.

"Git back!" he cried.

At the same time he reached out with his left hand and caught hold of Bickle. "No shooting, Bickle. You heard what the boss said."

"I'll kill 'im!" screamed Bickle, fighting to free himself from the other outlaw's grip.

"Give me a gun and you can try," Ralls invited. "Or put down your gun and I'll fight you with my fists."

Bickle shook off the other man's detaining grip and jumped at Ralls. But the momentary delay had restored some sanity to him and he did not shoot Ralls. He did, however, swing with the gun in his fist.

Ralls threw up his hands and took the first blow on his left forearm. Pain streaked up his arm, clear into his shoulders. He swung at Bickle with his fist, landed a solid blow in the stomach before Bickle could strike at him again.

He stepped aside, dodged a blow of the gun and was all set to smash the outlaw with a right hook, when one of the men lunged at him from behind. He landed in the small of Ralls' back, drove him forward into a flailing blow of Bickle's hand. The weapon exploded on his head and Ralls went down to his hands and knees. In that position he might have recovered, but the enraged Bickle stooped and clubbed him savagely with his gun. Ralls went down flat on his head, totally unconscious. But even then Bickle did not stop. He kicked Ralls in the side, turned him over with his feet and stamped three or four times on his face. He wound up with a terrific kick at Ralls' forehead.

A thousand little devils beat on Ralls' head with tiny sledgehammers and after a while they laid aside their sledges and picked up tongs, with which they tore at the nerve centers in Ralls' body.

That was more than any human could stand and Ralls groaned and rolled away from the little people. His eyes opened and winked shut again as pain streaked from his head clear down to his toes. He was conscious then, but afraid to move for fear of causing insufferable pain. Yet, after awhile, he called on his last reserves and forced open his eyes once more and looked up at a myriad of stars and a moon that was almost full and was high in the heavens.

He lay for minutes just staring at the sky and wondering why he was still alive.

A dull rhythmical thumping finally penetrated his senses and he strained his ears to determine the nature of the sound. It came closer and he suddenly realized that it was the clumping of a man's boots, very near.

He let his eyes go shut and the boots came up beside him and stopped. Ralls knew that eyes were looking down at him. A boot touched him and he had to fight to control an involuntary movement, but was rewarded by hearing a grunt. The boots moved off, continued thumping for awhile, then faded away, altogether.

Ralls opened his eyes again and rolled his head slightly to the right. He saw only shadows and turned to the left. A square shadow met his eyes and after focusing on it a moment, he made out that it was the log cabin in which Sage was reposing at the moment. At least, he hoped she was in it.

This was the spot where Bickle had clubbed him to insensibility. They had either given him up for dead or were too lazy to move him into the second cabin. Ralls looked again at the moon and decided from its position that it was after midnight, which meant that he had been unconscious at least six hours. And possibly eight or nine.

Gritting his teeth, Ralls began flexing his muscles. The effort brought out perspiration over his body, but when he finished flexing he began moving his toes, then his knees and finally his thighs. Satisfied that no bones were broken, he tried his fingers, hands and finally arms.

He was covered with bruises, some of them welts of pain, but was apparently still sound of limb. He rested a few minutes then, listening for the steps of the sentinel, but when he did not hear them he drew a deep breath and sat up. From that position he searched his surroundings and, seeing no signs of life, got noiselessly to his feet. Picking his steps carefully, he walked to the farther of the two buildings.

The door stood open and he turned his face sidewards, in a listening position. Rhythmical snoring assailed his ears. Satisfied, he moved softly to the other cabin, but even though he pressed his ear to the door, heard no sound of life inside.

He ran his fingernails lightly over the rough wooden door, listened a moment, then scratched again, slightly louder. And at last relief flooded through him. There was a creaking sound inside.

Ralls tapped on the door with his fingertips, as lightly as he could, but persistently. He stopped after awhile and listened. He thought he heard a faint slithering inside the cabin, but could not be sure. He tapped again, once or twice. A tiny creaking came from within.

Ralls put his face close to the door and said softly: "Sage . . . !"

There was a slight pause, then her voice responded almost breathlessly, "Yes?"

"It's Ralls . . ."

He could hear her inhale sharply. "I thought you were—"

"I'm all right," Ralls said quickly. "Can you open the door—without making any noise?"

"I'll try."

He heard her fumbling inside with a wooden bar, felt rather then heard it thump as she set it down beside the door. Then as the door was pulled open an inch or two, to the accompaniment of a squeak, Ralls' eager fingers caught the door and continued its opening, a half inch at a time. When the opening was large enough, Sage's face appeared.

"I'm going to try to get outside," Ralls whispered.

"They've got guards posted," Sage protested quickly.

"I know, there's one walking around here somewhere—and two more at the pass. But I can't wait until morning." He hesitated. "And I don't think you can."

"Dorcas wouldn't harm me."

"Don't be too sure of that."

Sage was silent a moment, then she shook her head. "I—I can't help being worried, but you don't know that Dorcas is—well, working for my father."

"I know that. That's why I say you'd better leave with me—now."

Sage started to exclaim, but Ralls reached out quickly and covered her mouth with his hand. Only for a moment. Then he took it away and stepped back.

Sage said, with quiet indignation, "You're suggesting that my father . . . ?"

"I'm not suggesting anything," Ralls cut in. "You've had plenty of time to think things over."

"Yes, I have."

"And do you think you'd be safe with Dorcas?" Ralls waited a moment and when she did not reply, he added: "You opened the door to me a moment ago. And you weren't asleep when I scratched on the door."

Sage drew a deep breath and took hold of the door. But Ralls caught it first and opened it wider. Sage stepped to the ground and winced a little as she stepped on a stone.

"My boots."

"Get them," Ralls said, "for we're going to walk a long ways."

She re-entered the cabin and Ralls stepped away. His

head was cocked to one side in a listening attitude. Some distance away a boot scraped a rock.

Like a shadow Ralls moved back to the doorway and, reaching inside, groped for the wooden door bar. His fingers found it, a flattened pole perhaps three inches thick and four wide.

Sage materialized out of the darkness and Ralls said, as softly as he could: "Somebody's coming. Wait here . . . !"

She froze instantly and Ralls took a cautious step along the side of the cabin. The tramping of boots on gravel became more distinct and suddenly a tall figure loomed up in the moonlight. It came along deliberately, unsuspectingly.

Then, suddenly, ten feet from the log cabin, the guard came to a halt. He was expecting to see something on the ground: Jim Ralls; and he wasn't there.

Ralls hurtled out of the shadows toward the guard. The man jumped back. A cry of alarm began in his throat and was crushed as Ralls struck with the wooden bar, a hard, savage blow. The man crumpled like a stricken rabbit and Ralls dropped quickly to his knees and, groping at the man's belt, found a revolver. With it in his hand, he turned and came to his feet.

He remained still, then, half expecting someone to emerge from the other cabin. But moments went by and there was only silence, so Ralls moved back to Sage's cabin.

She appeared out of the darkness. "All right?"

"I've got his gun," Ralls said. "But I don't think I dare go into the other cabin. There are four of them and if a shot is fired, the men at the pass will hear it. We'd never get through."

Sage shivered. "Let's get away from here. I—I'm scared."

"For that matter," said Ralls, "so am I."

He reached out and took her arm. For a moment her flesh stiffened under his hand, but then she relaxed and stepped out to the ground.

He led her forty or fifty feet away behind the cabin, then stopped. "Wait, I'll be right back."

She started to object, but he was already gliding away in the darkness. He returned to the cabin, groped until he came upon the body of the man he had felled, stooped, and smashed down on the man's head, with the barrel of the captured revolver. A groan came from the man and Ralls struck again. Straightening, he went swiftly back to Sage.

"I—I heard what you did," she said, shuddering.

"I had to," Ralls said. "We've got to get by two men and if he recovered consciousness and called out, we'd never make it."

"I realize that," Sage said. "Still . . ." She left her thought unexpressed.

He took her arm again and they started cautiously toward the pass an eighth of a mile or so distant, where they could expect to find another guard.

They had traveled but a short distance when Sage said: "This may sound silly, but I've a feeling that I've been in this valley before."

"Perhaps you have."

"No, I haven't, yet . . ." She paused a moment. "I have the strangest feeling of—I don't know how to express it, but, well, as if something dreadful is about to happen to me. I—I've felt that way ever since I was brought in here today."

"Those cabins," Ralls said, "are pretty old, twenty years or more."

"Nobody lived here twenty years ago," Sage said. "Dad was the first settler and he came in 1857."

"Seventeen years ago. You were four, then."

"How did you know?"

"You're twenty-one, aren't you?"

"Yes, but I don't remember telling you."

"You didn't; somebody else told me."

"Who?"

Ralls pressed her arm for silence as they had approached rather close to the incline that led up to the inner pass. "Get ready to freeze," he whispered.

They proceeded carefully another fifty feet or so, then came to a tree. Ralls indicated that Sage should kneel behind it. Standing beside her so that his body seemed to blend with the trunk in the shadows, he listened for long moments. But if there was any sound other than the night chirping of insects his ears failed to detect it. Yet—he would have sworn that someone was not too far away. He got it, then, a faint whiff of tobacco smoke. Someone was smoking a cigarette nearby.

"Careful," he breathed into Sage's ear. "Don't make any sudden movement."

Nineteen

HE STOOPED and, groping on the ground, found a couple of small pebbles. Straightening, he threw one in the direction of the rocks ahead. It made but a faint clatter, but instantly a shadow appeared about forty feet to the front and left of Ralls and Sage.

A faint glow of fire indicated a burning cigarette in the guard's mouth. With that to guide him, Ralls could have shot the man, but a shot at this point would spell disaster for them.

The man ahead walked forward a few yards, then turned and made a circle that became more careless as he progressed and satisfied himself that his ears had played him false. He stopped and stood for a moment, silhouetted in the moonlight perhaps forty feet from Ralls, then suddenly dropped out of sight as he again seated himself on the ground with a boulder to support his back.

Ralls stooped slightly and putting his lips so close to Sage's ear that they brushed, he whispered: "I'll have to get him. You wait here."

He felt a shiver of apprehension run through her body, but she did not speak. Ralls seated himself on the ground, took off his right boot and laid it carefully on the ground. Then he took off the other and, bending forward, moved ahead on hands and knees, one hand placed carefully on the ground, then the other. A knee moved forward, the other, then a hand.

It took him ten minutes to cover twenty-five of the forty feet. Then he paused and took his bearings. The boulder behind which the guard sat was about a dozen feet ahead of him. The cigarette smoke was strong in Ralls' nostrils.

He moved forward again, a foot, two, and up to the boulder itself. All he had to do now was get to his feet, reach over and strike the man unconscious with a single blow. He could not miss or hit a glancing blow, for in the stillness of the night an outcry would reach the guard on the outside of the pass, not more than an eighth of a mile away.

He drew up one knee, raised it and placed his socked foot carefully upon the ground.

Then a ripple of horror raced through Ralls, for the guard on the other side of the rock suddenly got to his feet. In his awkward position Ralls became as stiff and motionless as a statue, his eyes glued upon the man less than three feet from him.

The man did not turn. The cigarette was gone from his lips and he muttered something under his breath and reached into his pockets. It took Ralls a moment to realize that he was fishing out the makings, preparatory to rolling a fresh cigarette.

Quickly, Ralls determined the instant for his move. The man's mind was occupied at the moment, yet he was in a position where he could move quickly if he suspected that something was wrong.

Ralls controlled his breathing. He waited with one foot on the ground, resting on his other knee and both hands.

The man on the other side of the rock made small movements, then reached up with one hand and into his pocket with the other. The match. The striking of it and the tiny sputtering that would follow would mask Ralls' rise from the ground.

The man brought something out of his pocket, whipped it along the side of his trousers, muttered and repeated the movement. A flame appeared and was moved quickly upwards.

Ralls rose. In the same movement he whipped out the revolver he had taken from the first guard and lunged across the three-foot boulder. He could not miss. The match before the man's face silhouetted his head.

Ralls struck and bone crunched under the gun. There was no outcry and the man's body did not even fall, for Ralls swarmed over the rock and caught it as it was falling. He lowered it gently to the ground and stood for a moment, shaking in tremendous relief. He knew that his face was filmed with perspiration.

Two down and one more to go!

A foot scraping on rock caused Ralls to whirl. It was Sage coming forward. He went to meet her. She thrust something at him, his boots. He took them, seated himself on the ground, pulled them on. Rising, he said:

"All right."

"I know," she whispered. "But I almost fainted when he suddenly got up in front of you."

Ralls exhaled heavily. "We've got to move. The moon's getting pretty well along and it'll be daylight in a couple more hours."

She took his arm this time, but finding it awkward to walk behind him, slipped her hand down to meet his. He gripped it firmly and guided her along.

The going was more difficult here, for the room was obscured as they entered the cleft in the rock that afforded the actual passage into the hidden valley. And in the ravines on the other side there were trees they had to travel

through, which obscured the ground so that they stepped
on twigs on several occasions and had to halt to determine
that the third guard was not coming to investigate. Also,
Ralls had no idea where the man would be posted. He
might be in one of the two ravines, or he might be out on
the main slope of the mountain that overlooked Horseshoe
Valley. Fear nagged them, too. Ralls believed that he had
effectively disposed of the first two guards inside the
valley, yet one of the four outlaws in the cabin might wake
up, go outside and discover the first guard and raise the
alarm. A single shot fired in the valley would put the man
ahead on the alert.

They traversed the first ravine, covered the rocky ground
to the second and waited there for precious moments while
Ralls' sharp eyes investigated every suspicious shadow.
Finally they moved forward again slowly, carefully, and
emerged upon the outer slope of the mountain.

The guard had to be here. Forcing Sage down to the
ground in the shadow of a small shrub, Ralls went forward
several feet. He stooped and picked up a couple of small
stones. He threw one down the slope so that it landed sixty
or seventy feet away.

And then a low chuckle broke the stillness of the night.
It came from the right of Ralls, above. Ralls whirled, his
hand snaking for the gun in his holster.

Thunder and lightning split the night. Fire seared the left
side of Ralls under his armpit. But then he was firing at
the spot from where the flash had come. Two, three, four
times!

Steel clattered on stone and Ralls ran up the slope. He
found the guard flat on his face; near by lay a Winchester
repeating rifle.

Ralls stooped to touch the man, encountered a mass of
gristle and warm blood. Wiping his hand on the ground,
he picked up the Winchester and was turning when Sage
came running toward him.

Ralls stepped in front of the dead man so she would not see him. "We've got to run for it now," he said.

"They'll have horses."

"I know, but it'll be some minutes before they come out. The shots have awakened them, but they'll spend a few minutes talking about it and searching for the first man. They'll find him then and run to the pass—or call for the second guard. When they don't hear from him, they'll saddle horses. We'll have eight or ten minutes before they come out here."

Ralls' eyes searched the open valley that lay below them. The moonlight lit it up much too brightly to suit him. He shook his head.

"If I remember right, there isn't any cover for a couple of miles, perhaps more." He turned and looked up the mountain slope. "I wonder if it wouldn't be better to climb."

"No!" exclaimed Sage. "Up there we'll be cut off when daylight comes."

"They haven't got enough men to make a thorough search."

"But our men don't ride up there. Out in the valley we've got a chance."

"You think you'll be safe if we encounter an H-L man?"

"Of course." She searched his face in the moonlight. "You hinted at that before. What do you mean?"

"I think it would be a mistake for you to return to the H-L."

"That's ridiculous."

"All right," Ralls said. "I hope I'm wrong. But we can't stay here any longer." He took her hand, started quickly down the mountain slope.

They spent five minutes descending to the floor of the valley. Then Ralls drew a deep breath and releasing Sage's hand, said: "We'll have to run—as long as you can run."

Sage responded by breaking into a sprint. Ralls followed, running easily at her side. They went a half mile when Ralls detected that Sage's breath was laboring. He slackened to a walk.

"We'll have to save a little."

He looked over his shoulder searching the mountainside they had vacated but saw no signs of life. He had not expected any yet.

"There ought to be a cottonwood grove around here somewhere," Sage panted.

"There is," Ralls said. "Bend low and look ahead a little to the right. You'll see it silhouetted against the moon."

Still walking, Sage crouched low and scanned the horizon. "I see it, but it's so far away."

"Three miles, I figure," Ralls said grimly.

Sage began running again, and Ralls trotted beside her. But when his own breathing became difficult he reached out and pulled Sage down to a walk.

They were a mile from the mountainside, more than two from the shelter of the cottonwood grove. A faint sound came to Ralls' ears.

"They're out," he announced.

A sob caught in Sage's throat. "We've got to run."

"You can't," Ralls said flatly.

He pulled her down to the ground. "The grass is more than a foot high; they'd have to come pretty close before they'd see us. And I've got a rifle."

Lying flat in the grass, with Sage struggling for breath beside him, Ralls scanned the ground before him. Unfortunately the mountain behind them prevented the outlaws from being silhouetted against the skyline, but in a little while, by pressing his ear to the ground, he heard the drumming of horses' hoofs and knew that the outlaws were on the search for them. They were coming fast, too. They knew the ground ahead of them.

After a moment Ralls began to wonder if it was not fortunate for him and Sage that they had not reached the cottonwood grove. The outlaws knew about it and seemed to be heading for it as fast as their horses could take them. They would scour it thoroughly.

He reached out and found Sage's shoulders. "They're heading for the cottonwoods and I think they're going to pass very near."

The pounding of the horses' hoofs became louder and Ralls raised his head a few inches to peer above the grass. He saw them then, four riders spread out so they covered more than a hundred yards of ground. The two horsemen on the right were in line with Ralls and Sage.

He lowered his head to the ground. "Steady," he cautioned Sage. But he gripped his rifle with his right hand, even pushed it ahead a few inches so he could throw it up quickly.

The thunder of the galloping horses rose to a crescendo and became so frightening that Ralls had to grit his teeth to control himself, keep himself lying flat on the ground. For one terrifying moment he was certain that iron-shod hoofs would crush the life from his body, but then a clod of earth, spurned by a flying hoof, struck the back of his head and the danger was over. Rapidly the pounding became less and in another moment or two Ralls squirmed around on the ground and, raising his head, saw the open formation of horsemen between them and the island of cottonwoods two miles away.

Sage said in tremendous relief, "I was never so scared in my life."

Ralls exhaled. "You can relax—for awhile."

"You mean we have to stay here?"

"I see no alternative. Not for some time. They'll beat

those woods until daylight and when they don't find us they'll run back and forth out here on the range. I doubt if they'll find us, though. The longer we keep out of sight the better our chances will get."

Twenty

IN THE early dawn, before the sun rose over the mountain range, Roy Dorcas strode out of the Langford ranch house. His features were set in a savage mask as he strode toward the corrals, where a dozen cowpunchers were saddling up their horses.

As he walked across the ranch yard he picked out Emmett Langford and shifted his course so that he came up to him. Emmett turned from tightening a saddle cinch.

"Hello, Uncle," he said sarcastically.

"You young whelp," Dorcas said angrily. "I told you last night there'd be no riding this morning."

"Why," Emmett said coolly, "I thought things over during the night and decided that *I* was going to run things around here."

Dorcas raised his hand and struck Emmett in the face with his open palm, a hard, stinging blow. "Do something about that," Dorcas raged. "And this . . . !" He followed through with a second blow.

Emmett reeled back, mouthing incoherent curses. He clawed at his six-gun, but before he could draw it, Sam Sloane stepped up and pushed him aside.

"I'll take over, Bad Man," Sloane sneered.

"Keep out of this, Sloane," Dorcas warned.

"I couldda told *you* that," Sloane said nastily. "Pick on a kid who ain't dry behind the ears. Well, *I'm* your size, Dorcas, so go ahead, draw any time you feel lucky."

Emmett, who had recovered somewhat by this time, came up beside Sloane. "This is the showdown, Dorcas."

Feet came pounding from the direction of the bunk-houses. Out of the corner of his eye Dorcas recognized his men, three case-hardened veterans of the quick draw and the hard ride. There were a dozen H-L men here. Dorcas did not think he could count on any of them. But he decided to make an attempt.

"Look here, Emmett," he said loudly. "I'm Harley Langford's brother—"

"And I'm his son," Emmett snapped.

"His adopted son," Dorcas corrected. "And there's a big difference."

"There ain't a damn bit of difference," Emmett retorted. "Besides which the old man said I was to run things."

"That's a lie," cried Dorcas. "He didn't say anything of the kind. He said—"

"Callin' me a liar!" blustered Emmett, trying to force the issue.

Dorcas sent a quick glance about the corral. There wasn't a man paying any attention to his horse. All the H-L men, as well as Dorcas' own three riders, were poised, waiting for the blowup that seemed certain to come. But there was no alignment of forces, nothing definite to indicate how the H-L men would fight, for or against Emmett Langford.

Then Reb Jenkins pushed forward. "Look here, Emmett," he said, "you don't want to start a fight—"

"Keep out of this!" Emmett warned.

"I will like hell," Reb said. "I'm still the ramrod of this spread and I'm warning you I'll not pull a gun *for* you." He looked quickly about the group. "Not in a setup like this. And I don't think the boys will either."

Emmett took a quick step to the side, looked deliberately about the ring of faces—and saw no encouragement. He whirled on Dorcas. "Get out of here!" he choked. "Climb the hell on a horse and get off this ranch."

"I think Harley'll have something to say about that."

Emmett circled Roy Dorcas, cutting him off from a direct line to the ranch house. "Ride!" he cried.

Sam Sloane shuffled over to Emmett's side, his thumbs hooked in his belt, a mocking, inviting smile on his lips.

Dorcas hesitated; the issue was still in doubt, but he wasn't inclined to force it at the moment. He had lived a long time by the gun because he was instinctively a cautious man and fought only when the odds were in his favor.

He signaled to his men and they got horses and saddled them. Then the four outlaws rode slowly from the H-L Ranch. When they were some distance from the house, Emmett Langford strode up to Reb Jenkins. "Now you can get your horse, Reb. You're through here."

"The old man hired me and he'll fire me," Reb retorted.

"You've got one minute to get a horse saddled and moving," Emmett said. "Sam, start counting."

Reb Jenkins was in the saddle with seconds to spare. Emmett faced the cowpunchers then. "Anybody else want to know who's boss around here?" he demanded.

The question had been settled to the cowpunchers' entire satisfaction, although none spoke a word. "Climb in your saddles, then," Emmett ordered. "We're riding today and by the time we come back tonight there'll be only one ranch in the valley, the H-L."

Fourteen H-L riders, including Emmett Langford and Sam Sloane, lined up in the lush grass of Horseshoe Valley, a quarter of a mile from the ranch buildings of the Allison Ranch. The buildings were of fair size, but small when compared to the ones on the H-L Ranch.

Emmett Langford, like a cavalry general, rode out in front of his men and surveyed the line of battle.

"All right, men," he said, "you know what to do. Every building, every corral, right down to the ground."

Sam Sloane suddenly rode his horse forward. "Now wait a minute, Emmett," he said. "I'm not arguing with you about who's boss, but I don't like this, riding down in the open. They'll pick off half of us before we get in revolver range."

Emmett Langford smiled. "Who, the Chinese cook?"

Sam Sloane looked past Emmett, toward the ranch buildings. "I don't see anyone around, but they may be sleeping late this morning."

"They're not sleeping," Emmett said. "They rode out at dawn."

"How do you know?"

Emmett hesitated. "I made a deal."

Sloane exclaimed, "With Cagle—last night?"

Emmett nodded. "Allison, at seven o'clock, Rudabaugh at eight and Macfadden at nine. There won't be a man at any of the places."

Sam Sloane began to chuckle. "All right, chief, I'll be right behind you."

He eased his horse back into the line. Emmett gathered up his bridle reins. "Let's go!" he cried and spurred his horse toward the ranch buildings ahead.

A wild shout rose from the fourteen cowboys as they charged forward at full speed. When they were halfway to the ranch house a man with a pigtail flying behind him darted out of the cook shack and headed for the rambling ranch house.

A cowpuncher let fly at him with a bullet. Whooping, other men began firing and bullets kicked up dirt all around the Chinese cook. And then, suddenly, he broke in his stride and pitched to the ground on his face.

The cowboys swarmed down upon the ranch buildings,

riddling them with bullets, but there was no answering fire and not another human came out of the buildings.

The H-L men dismounted and began dashing into buildings. Soon smoke was pouring out of the windows and doors. Several men threw lassos over the corral poles, pulled them loose and dragged them toward blazing buildings.

They spent not over fifteen minutes at the Allison Ranch, but when they rode off the ranch buildings were a mass of fire and smoke.

Leaving the Allison place, the H-L men, with Emmett Langford and Sam Sloane at their head, rode across country in the direction of the Rudabaugh spread some five or six miles away. Smoke from Allison's could be seen there, but that didn't matter. The Rudabaugh men, along with Allison's and Macfadden's, were all at Meadowlands, twelve miles in the opposite direction. They would be held there, too; that was Cagle's deal with Emmett Langford.

The Rudabaugh Ranch was reached in good time. It was a larger, more impressive place than the ranch that had been Allison's. There was a pretty good-sized ranch house set at the end of a lane of transplanted cottonwoods. The bunkhouses and stables were on alternate sides behind the cottonwoods, so that you rode between them as you approached the ranch house; actually the buildings were a good two hundred yards apart, however.

Emmett didn't line up his men this time. The moment the ranch was sighted, his men put their horses into a trot and even passed the leaders, Emmett and Sloane. Which is what saved their lives. For the Rudabaugh ranch was an ambush. There were no men in the open, but in the bunkhouses and stables were almost twenty men, all armed with rifles.

The H-L men, charging down the line between the buildings, were perfect targets. There was a good commander with the Rudabaugh forces, too, for he withheld the fire of his command until the majority of the H-L men were whooping down the line. Then he gave the orders and a withering volley was fired from both sides.

Five saddles were emptied in that first fire. Two more men went down a moment later and the others scattered. The Rudabaugh men poured out of the buildings and began firing after them. Four more men were brought down. Only two, aside from Sloane and Emmett, got away. The latter pair, actually, did not come into the fire, for being passed by the charging cowboys they were fifty yards behind the trap and at the first volley they whirled their horses and, bending low in the saddles, rode for their lives.

Les Cagle had made a deal with Emmett Langford—to double-cross him. The Allison's ranch buildings had been sacrificed, yes, but it was a small price to pay. Allison would no doubt receive recompense in some form; perhaps another double cross.

Two miles from the scene of the debacle, Sam Sloane caught up with Emmett Langford. Emmett's face was drained of blood and there was a wild look in his eyes. Sloane yelled at him to pull up his horse but the young gun-slinger didn't even seem to hear. Then Sloane forced his own animal up close to Emmett's and leaning over grabbed the bridle reins and brought both horses to a halt.

"They'll be after us," Emmett cried.

Sloane slapped Emmett's face with the palm of his hand, then brought the hand back and gave Emmett the knuckles.

"I should have had my head examined when I let a young pup like you give me orders," Sloane snarled.

"Cagle double-crossed me!"

"Sure, he double-crossed you. You should have expected that. This is a man's game and the chips are all blue. This was a good setup and you let it slide out from under us.'' Sloane drew a deep breath. ''Now, I've got to start riding again.''

''I'll go with you, Sam!''

''You!'' Sloane jeered at Emmett. ''I need you about as much as I need a hump on my back.''

''I can shoot,'' Emmett declared. ''And I can draw as fast as any man. You said so yourself.''

''Sure I said it,'' Sloane retorted mockingly. ''That was when I was drawing your old man's pay.'' He sneered. ''You really think you can draw a gun?''

He raised his hands level with his shoulders. ''Go ahead, draw . . .''

Emmett wiped saliva from his mouth with the back of his hand. ''There ain't many men can beat you, Sam . . .''

''There ain't none!''

''. . . Except Ralls. . . .''

''Ralls!'' exclaimed Sam Sloane. ''He's supposed to have beat a lot of men, but who ever saw him do it? Man drygulches somebody, shoots him when he isn't lookin' and he builds himself a reputation. Me, I've faced the best there was and I'm still here. And I'll be around a long time after Ralls is buried.''

''Ralls is dead by now. Or he will be in a little while.''

''How do you know?''

''Dorcas. He's left. When he doesn't show up at the hideout, do you think Bickle will let Ralls ride away?''

''What about the girl?''

''Her, too.''

Sloane scowled at Emmett. ''You're a no-good bastard, aren't you, Emmett?''

''Like you said a minute ago, the chips are blue.''

Sloane's eyes screwed up in thought. ''Dorcas is gone and most of his men. And Ralls won't show up again. Or the girl. That leaves your old man—and us.''

''Against Cagle and all the other ranchers.''

A wicked grin twisted Sloane's mouth. ''And how long

do you think they'll be friends? Sure, they ganged up on your father, because he was strong enough to lick them all, unless they stuck together. But they figure the H-L don't count anymore. They'll be looking out for themselves now. . . ." He licked his lips with his tongue. "A good man, hidin' out and pickin' off a man once in awhile, could play hell with them. They don't trust each other and each one'll figure the other's after them. . . ."

"Two good men could do a better job, Sam," cried Emmett.

Sloane hesitated. "One good man . . . and a cub. . . ."

"All right, Sam. You can run things. But I'll ride with you. And I'll show you that I can shoot with the best of them. I'll show you!"

Twenty-one

RAISING his head from the ground, Jim Ralls watched the oncoming rider. He was perhaps two hundred yards away and was making a large circle that would bring him at the closest point to within a hundred feet of Ralls and Sage. The rider was leaning over to the right, his eyes studying the ground as he searched for tracks.

Far beyond the rider, also traveling in a circle, was another horseman. And off to the right, a mile or more, a third man circled the range.

"We've got a few minutes," Ralls said to Sage. Then he exclaimed, "That's my horse he's riding!"

Sage's head came up involuntarily. "I thought your horse was a black gelding."

"Your beloved foster brother shot that one yesterday. This is the animal I used as a pack horse. Really a swifter horse than the gelding. Get down . . . !"

Sage ducked her head down to the ground and Ralls thrust out his Winchester. He rose deliberately to one knee and took aim. At that instant the horseman spotted Ralls and sent a quick revolver shot at him, which missed by yards.

Ralls pressed the trigger. The outlaw pitched from the

saddle, with a hoarse cry. Instantly Ralls sprang to his feet and, placing two fingers in his mouth, whistled shrilly.

The horse that had just lost its rider in the act of sheering away stopped dead in its tracks and threw up its head. Ralls whistled again and the animal came toward him at a gallop.

While it was bearing down Ralls looked beyond and saw the second horseman now coming toward him. He ejected the shell from the chamber of the Winchester and pumped in a fresh one.

Ralls' horse pounded up and, pawing the earth, neighed in recognition.

"Stay down," Ralls said to Sage. "I'm going to take care of Number Two."

The second outlaw was a quarter of a mile away, bearing down swiftly. Ralls stood to one side of his horse, the rifle at the ready. Four hundred yards. Three hundred.

The advancing outlaw began to pull up his horse. Then Ralls threw the rifle up to his shoulder, fired and quickly pumped in a new shell. He fired again, whether it was the first or second shot that did it he never knew, but the result was satisfactory. The horse was suddenly riderless.

Ralls stepped forward, caught the bridle reins of his horse and, turning, signaled to Sage, already rising from the grass. "Up you go!"

"But you . . ."

"I'll hold off the third man," Ralls said. "You get that other horse."

The order satisfied Sage and Ralls, holding his hands as a stirrup, raised her into the saddle of his horse. She took hold of the reins, whirled the animal and sent it racing after the riderless horse that was trotting away aimlessly.

Ralls turned, saw the third outlaw still more than a half mile away and decided to keep him at a distance. He sent a rifle bullet singing in the general direction of the man. It was enough of a warning for the man who had already seen two of his comrades unhorsed. He did not retreat, but remained at a distance of a half mile, just beyond effective rifle range.

Ralls began walking after Sage. He had confidence that she would catch the second horse and wanted to save as much time as possible.

A few minutes later he saw her ride down the loose animal, catch up the bridle reins, turn and come toward him. Ralls ran forward to meet her.

He vaulted into the saddle but before starting off, turned to look back. The outlaw was still maintaining a safe distance, but another horseman was riding from the direction of the mountain range to join him. That took care of the fourth man.

He said to Sage: "You're determined to go back to the H-L?"

She exclaimed, "There you go again! I think it's time you told me just what you've been driving at."

"Perhaps it *is* time you knew. It was Emmett who shot his father."

Sage stared at him in angry disbelief. "That's ridiculous!"

Ralls shook his head. "No more ridiculous than Harley Langford shooting *your* father."

"What?"

"Harley Langford isn't your father."

"Now you *are* crazy."

"I've got it figured out," Ralls said. "I may not be straight in everything, but I'm pretty close. Harley is Emmett's father, but not yours."

"It's exactly the other way. Emmett is the foster child. I—I'm Sage Langford. Not adopted, not foster . . ."

"How old is Emmett?"

"Twenty-three."

"And you?"

"Twenty-one. But I don't see—"

"Harley Langford picked up Emmett after the Mountain Meadows Massacre. That's his story, isn't it?"

"Yes, but . . ." Sage frowned. "You'll be telling me next that Dad was one of the murderers."

"No, he wasn't one of the Mormons who participated in the Massacre. Nor did he pick up Emmett there."

They were riding by this time, at a fast walk, side by side. Sage looked over her shoulder, then sidewards at Ralls. "You seem to know quite a lot about the Mountain Meadows Massacre."

"I know more about it than any man living. I've spent at least five years running down the history of the victims— and also the perpetrators. I haven't finished the job, but I don't think I'll have to. I'm certain enough that neither Emmett nor your father were within two hundred miles of Mountain Meadows, at the time of the Massacre, or immediately afterwards. They were right here in this valley."

"And where was I?"

Ralls was silent for a moment. Then he said: "Last night you said that you had a strange feeling that you'd been in Hidden Valley before. I think you were—seventeen years ago."

"With whom?"

"That's one of the points I'm not certain about. I may never know for sure unless—"

"Unless what?"

". . . Harley Langford talks. Or maybe Roy Dorcas. He knows."

Sage exclaimed, "He knows what?"

"The whole story."

Sage shook her head in bewilderment. "I don't know what you're talking about. I'm so confused I—I don't think I know anything."

"Maybe I can help to clear things up for you. What do

you remember about your childhood? Your earliest recol-
lections?''

''I remember Dad, of course. And the ranch . . .''

''Do you recall your mother?''

''I don't know. I sometimes get an image of someone
. . . a—a tired-looking woman.''

''Tired? You were going to use another adjective.''

''Frightened? All right, that's the image I always get
about her. She was afraid and—and crying. Always . . .
she was crying. And then the image fades away.'' She
suddenly looked over her shoulder. ''Last night the image
was the clearest of all. There in the dark, when you left me
for a moment to—to go after that second guard. It was
almost as clear as if the scene was happening then.
Mother—if it was mother—was crying and running. Then
she fell. But first there was a—a loud noise . . .''

''A gun?'' Ralls suggested.

''I—I don't know. That could have been suggested
because I was expecting, or dreading, to hear you shoot at
that man. But—the scene was the same. The two cabins,
the walls of the mountain looming over us on all sides
and—and mother.''

She stopped and they rode in silence a moment. Sage's
chin dropped.

Ralls said softly: ''You don't remember any father other
than . . . Harley Langford?''

She made no answer for a moment. Then she suddenly
shook her head.

''Do you remember when Emmett first came to live
with you?''

''Yes. That's one thing I do remember clearly. We were
living alone, Dad and I and . . .'' She stopped and her
head came up. Ralls, looking covertly at her, saw that her
eyes were squinting in thought.

''I almost said Uncle, but that couldn't be right, because
I have no uncle.''

"When you started to say Uncle did a picture of someone come into your mind?" Ralls asked quickly.

"N-no . . ." Sage winced and exclaimed, "I'm too confused. A picture *did* come before my eyes, but that's impossible. It was that outlaw leader, Roy Dorcas."

"That's it!" exclaimed Ralls. "It *was* Dorcas!"

"Are you saying that Roy Dorcas is my *uncle?*"

"No, but I *am* saying that he's Harley Langford's brother. I should have tumbled before. There's a certain family resemblance there. Not much, but enough. Dorcas' face kept bothering me. That was because I'd met Harley Langford first. And Hidden Valley—Dorcas knew about it. He told me that people around here couldn't find it in a day's search, even if they knew about where to look for it. But Dorcas knew—because he'd been in the valley before. Twenty years ago, or—seventeen."

"Jim!" Sage cried out. "Look . . . !"

For one of the few times in his life Ralls had been caught napping. But he had been so intent in his exposition that he had been watching Sage instead of the valley ahead. Now at Sage's exclamation he looked up and saw— Roy Dorcas!

Dorcas and three riders coming toward them, and less than a hundred yards away. Not far behind them was a grove of trees, out of which they had evidently ridden.

Ralls raised the Winchester, but stopped. Roy Dorcas' right hand had gone up, palm toward him in the Indian gesture of friendship or parley.

Ralls distrusted the outlaw chieftain, but the distance between them was small and behind were two more outlaws. Ralls was in no position for a duel, especially with Sage close beside him.

He pulled up his horse. "This may be bad. If there's a fight—run . . . !"

Dorcas' men halted their horses, but Dorcas himself

rode forward to within thirty feet of Ralls. For a moment Dorcas regarded Ralls bitterly: "So you got away!" His eyes went past Ralls to the two riders in the distance. "Is that all that's left?"

"Your string's about played out, Dorcas," Ralls said.

"I'm getting too old," Dorcas said. "I figure on pulling out tomorrow. Maybe I'll get me a farm somewhere in the East." His face twisted angrily. "But I'm going to finish here." His eyes shifted from Ralls to the face of Sage. "The business concerns you."

"Are you my uncle?" Sage suddenly shot at him.

Dorcas grimaced wryly. His eyes left Sage's face and came back to Ralls. "Just how much do you know, Ralls?"

"Most of it, maybe all."

"You've told her?"

"Not all. She—she doesn't want to believe it. For which I can't blame her. I had a hard time believing it myself."

"*Are* you my uncle?" Sage persisted.

"I'm not going to answer that question," Dorcas said. "It's up to—to Harley." He scowled. "The cub's gone crazy. Drove me off the ranch. He's got some wild scheme of wiping out everybody in the territory—"

"Including Harley Langford?" Ralls said.

"You really think he bushwhacked Harley?"

"Don't *you* think so?"

"Yes!" snapped Dorcas. "And I'm pretty sure Harley knows it, but he hates to admit it—even to himself. His own son."

Sage exclaimed, "Emmett *is* Dad's son—his *real* son?"

Dorcas cleared his throat in chagrin. But he wouldn't look at Sage. He said to Ralls: "You want to make a try for the ranch . . . with me and the boys?"

"Together?"

"You said yourself the game was up." He shrugged. "I'll give you my word—"

"Your word," said Ralls. Then added suddenly: "All right, I'll ride with you. But . . ." He jerked his thumb over his shoulders. "Tell those fellows to keep their distance."

Twenty-two

ON THE knoll overlooking the H-L ranch buildings, Ralls and Sage pulled up their horses. Behind them fifty yards, Dorcas also stopped. His men, reduced to five in number, were a quarter of a mile or more to the rear.

They had no stomach for riding down on the H-L, and preferred a safe distance between them and the ranch buildings. Dorcas had argued with them, but that was as far as they would come. "We'll cover you if you make a break," Bickle had growled at his chief, "but damned if I'll ride into a trap."

There were plenty of men about the H-L, but they were strange men. Not H-L riders. A couple of horsemen were approaching the little group on the knoll. They were armed with rifles and six-guns were prominent in their holsters.

While still some distance away, one of the approaching riders yelled out: "Keep away if you know what's good for you."

Ralls moved his horse ahead of the others. "Who's in charge?" he called out.

"What business is it of yours?" shouted one of the men in return. Then he pulled up his horse so suddenly the animal almost went back on its haunches. "Jim Ralls!"

"I want to talk to whoever's running the place," Ralls said quickly.

The two horsemen were shying away their horses, sidewards, toward the ranch buildings. Then almost as if at a signal, they both whirled and galloped back the way they had come.

Ralls, watching them, saw a man ride out toward them. The three had a quick parley, then the new man rode past the other two and came toward Ralls at a trot. When he approached, Ralls identified him as Les Cagle, wearing blue jeans, boots and gun belt, instead of his customary saloonkeeper's costume.

Cagle stopped a dozen yards away. "Thought you'd be out of this country by now."

"We want to talk to Harley Langford," Ralls said, "that is, if he's still alive."

"Oh, he's alive, all right, but don't you know what's happened?"

"You seem to have captured the H-L," Ralls said, "which doesn't surprise me too much. I rather thought you would."

Cagle chuckled. "That Emmett boy! Thought he was a regular Texas twister. Burned out the Allison spread this morning, then made a try for the Rudabaugh outfit. He didn't do so well."

"Dead?"

"One or two of the men got away, I think. They're probably crossing the Idaho line about now."

"So then you rode down here and took over?"

"Why not? That's what Langford planned to do to us." His eyes flickered past Ralls to where Sage and Roy Dorcas sat their horses. "What can you do with a crippled man?"

"I shouldn't think that would bother you—much."

"Bothers some of the boys. He's only got a day or two, anyway."

"Then you shouldn't mind our talking to him."

Again Cagle's eyes went past Ralls. "That's Roy Dorcas with you."

"He's Langford's brother."

"I know." Cagle chewed at his lower lip with his sharp, white teeth, then he suddenly signaled to the outlaw. "Dorcas!"

Dorcas came forward with Sage at his side. "Yes?" Dorcas said. Then his eyes widened. "Bert Needham!"

"Cagle's the name," the saloonkeeper said. "Les Cagle." He paused briefly. "Same as yours is Roy Dorcas."

"Why not, Cagle?"

Cagle shook his head. "This is my game, Roy. I've played my cards and I've won. I don't figure to replay the hand."

"I'm pulling out right after I talk to Harley."

"That's not good enough. I've an idea what you want to talk to Langford about—with Ralls here—and I think I'd kind of like you to have that talk with him. Might square up the edges a little. The only thing is—well, it's taken me quite awhile to play this hand. A good many years."

"Sure, Cagle," Dorcas said easily. "You don't have to draw a picture for me. You want me to keep my mouth shut in front of your people."

"And you'll give me your guns."

"No," Ralls said bluntly. "I gave up my gun yesterday."

"Then this is as far as you go, Ralls!"

"Guess again, Cagle."

Cagle's eyes became slits. "You can't win . . ."

"Call me, then."

"Damn you, Ralls, I should have shot you down the first time I laid eyes on you. You've given me nothing but trouble."

"You've given me a little, too. We're riding down, Cagle."

"Damn you to hell!" Then Cagle suddenly pulled himself together. "All right, but you may not ride out." He turned his horse and put it to a gallop.

Ralls, Dorcas and Sage were right on his heels and so they rode down to the ranch buildings. When they dismounted, Ralls kept within a pace or two of Cagle. Men stood around, watching them with hostile faces.

The door of the ranch house burst open and big Ben Rudabaugh stormed out. "Cagle!" he roared. "Who've you got there?"

"See for yourself," Cagle snarled.

Rudabaugh bared his teeth in a wolfish grin. "Come to have that fight, Ralls?"

"Keep away from me," Ralls warned.

Rudabaugh guffawed. "You walk into the lion's den and you tell the lion to keep away?" He clapped a huge hand on his thigh. "When'll it be? Now . . . ?"

Ralls dropped his hand to the butt of his revolver. "Stand aside, Rudabaugh, I'm going into the house."

"Let him in," Cagle said testily.

"You, too," Ralls nodded to Cagle.

Rudabaugh took a sidewards step. "Say, who's got who here?"

Cagle glared at him and slammed open the front door. He went through, Ralls crowding his heels and passing within a yard of Rudabaugh and half expecting the big man to lunge for him. But Rudabaugh was a little uneasy about things. When Sage and Dorcas followed Ralls into the house, Rudabaugh caught the swinging door and went in after them.

In the house, Cagle led the way to Harley Langford's bedroom. He entered, holding the door for the others. Sage ran past Ralls, then, into the room.

She started for the bed, but before she reached it, stopped.

Harley Langford, his face drawn and gray, stared at Sage. "Sage," he said.

"Dad!" cried Sage. She made a forward movement, but again caught herself.

Roy Dorcas said: "Ralls told her."

The face of Harley Langford twitched. "Just as well," he said tonelessly.

A sob was torn from Sage's throat. "It's true . . . you're not . . . my father . . . ?"

Behind Sage, Jim Ralls said harshly, "Your father was Rance Martindale. Your mother's maiden name was Helen Sutherland. Tom Sutherland—your uncle—was the best friend I ever had in this world."

"So that's why you've been hounding me all these years," Harley Langford said wearily. "Tom Sutherland put you up to it. But why . . . why didn't Sutherland himself . . . ?"

"He died in Virginia," Ralls said bleakly. "He died saving my life." He stopped. Sage was standing in front of him, her hands to her face, sobbing so that her entire body heaved.

Tears. Tears. Helen Martindale had wept too, and she had been killed. She had seen her husband murdered, knew the fate that was in store for her and had gone to it, weeping.

Ralls went on remorselessly: "You murdered Rance Martindale, Langford. You murdered him in cold blood and you killed his wife. For fifty thousand dollars in gold . . ."

Langford's face was twisted in anguish. "For fifty thousand," he said, "and this valley. Yes, Martindale found it. He'd already built this house when Roy . . ." He faltered. "When Roy and I came here to our old hideout. The law was after us and we stayed in the Hidden Valley for awhile. Then we came across this place and Martindale . . . well, he took us at our face value—gave us jobs . . ." He paused again. "He was going east to get a herd of cattle. I—I started out with him, but I came back in a little while . . . alone. The rest you know. I took over the ranch.''

At the door Ben Rudabaugh said suddenly: "But if you killed her father and mother, why didn't you kill Sage?"

Langford's eyes closed as if in pain, and Roy Dorcas answered. "That was the weak point in the scheme. Harley didn't want to ride with me any more. This place appealed to him, but Martindale had already lived here for three-four months. He was apparently the only man in the territory, but we couldn't be sure some Mormons or somebody hadn't come through here. They might not remember the man's face, but they'd remember that a man and his wife lived here and that they had a little girl . . .''

Harley Langford's eyes opened again. "That wasn't all of it. I—I couldn't hurt her. I had a boy myself back East. I brought him out here—"

"And raised him as your foster son and the girl as your real daughter," Ralls said. "Just in case somebody remembered. Tom Sutherland, for example . . .''

"Tom Sutherland," Langford repeated. "I never even heard of him.''

"The devil you didn't," Ralls said angrily. "You can't admit the truth to yourself even now . . . when you're on the verge of death. Sage . . .'' Ralls reached out and almost touched her, but caught himself. "Tell him what *you* remember—Hidden Valley, where he'd taken your mother . . .''

"Gawd!" exclaimed Ben Rudabaugh. "You mean he didn't kill her right away?"

"Ask him," Ralls said.

Harley Langford groaned. "I . . . all right, I fell in love with her. But she—"

Outside the window a gun roared. Glass crashed and Harley Langford cried out; the last sound he ever made.

Flame lanced again from outside the shattered window, but by that time Ralls had moved. But instead of going for his gun he used the precious split second to hurtle forward and knock Sage to the floor. He went down himself, but as he rose, he came up with his gun.

The gun outside fired the third time and pain burned through Ralls' left arm. Then his gun bucked and thundered and a man outside the window crumpled to the ground.

Ralls continued to the window, turning sidewards and hurtling through it bodily. He landed heavily on the ground outside, shot a quick look at the dead, staring eyes of young Emmett Langford on the ground, then scrambled up and started running for the edge of the house.

He was ten feet from it when Sam Sloane stepped out. Sam Sloane, gun fighter extraordinary. A cigarette was pasted to Sloane's lower lip and there was a gun in his fist.

"Ralls!" he said.

He fired and Ralls buckled forward. But even as he went down to his knees, Ralls fired. Once. The gun fell from Sam Sloane's hand and he started to sway. Ralls shot again and then he collapsed himself to his hands and knees.

But Sam Sloane was dead.

Ralls heard boots pounding and there was gunfire, he thought, gunfire somewhat muffled. But he remained on his hands and knees, staring at the little spot of ground in front of his eyes.

He was still in that position when Ben Rudabaugh laid a heavy hand on his shoulder.

"Ralls," he said, "you got Sloane. And Emmett."

"I suppose so," Ralls said. "I always do."

Rudabaugh stooped beside Ralls and tried to look into his face, but he couldn't because Ralls kept looking at the ground. "You're hit, man," Rudabaugh said in a tone that bordered on awe. Which was unusual for him. "You're hit bad."

"I'll live," said Ralls. "I've *got* to live. There's Cagle—"

"He's dead," Rudabaugh said. "He and Dorcas shot it out. Dorcas is dying . . ."

"Sage . . ."

"I'm here," Sage said. She came running forward and dropping to her knees beside Ralls, took a gentle grip on the arm nearest hers. "I'm here, Jim." After a moment, she added: "Always."

"All right," Ralls said, "then I'll make it."